JANE FIELD

MORE WILDSIDE CLASSICS

Please see www.wildsidepress.com for a complete list!

JANE FIELD

MARY E. WILKINS

WILDSIDE PRESS

JANE FIELD

This edition published 2005 by Wildside Press, LLC.
www.wildsidepress.com

CHAPTER I

Amanda Pratt's cottage-house was raised upon two banks above the road-level. Here and there the banks showed irregular patches of yellow-green, where a little milky-stemmed plant grew. It had come up every spring since Amanda could remember.

There was a great pink-lined shell on each side of the front door-step, and the path down over the banks to the road was bordered with smaller shells. The house was white, and the front door was dark green, with an old-fashioned knocker in the centre.

There were four front windows, and the roof sloped down to them; two were in Amanda's parlor, and two were in Mrs. Field's. She rented half of her house to Mrs. Jane Field.

There was a head at each of Amanda's front windows. One was hers, the other was Mrs. Babcock's. Amanda's old blond face, with its folds of yellow-gray hair over the ears and sections of the softly-wrinkled, pinky cheeks, was bent over some needle-work. So was Mrs. Babcock's, darkly dim with age, as if the hearth-fires of her life had always smoked, with a loose flabbiness about the jaw-bones, which seemed to make more evident the firm structure underneath.

Amanda was sewing a braided rug; her little veiny hands jerked the stout thread through with a nervous energy that was out of accord with her calm expression and the droop of her long slender body.

"It's pretty hard sewin' braided mats, ain't it?" said Mrs. Babcock.

"I don't care how hard 'tis if I can get 'em sewed strong," replied Amanda, and her voice was unexpectedly quick and decided. "I never had any feelin' that anything was hard, if I could only do it."

"Well, you ain't had so much hard work to do as some folks. Settin' in a rockin'-chair sewin' braided mats ain't like doin' the housework for a whole family. If you'd had the cookin' to do for four men-folks, the way I have, you'd felt it was pretty hard work, even if you did make out to fill 'em up." Mrs. Babcock smiled, and showed that she did not forget she was company, but her tone was quite fierce.

"Mebbe I should," returned Amanda, stiffly.

There was a silence.

"Let me see, how many mats does that make?" Mrs. Babcock asked, finally, in an amiable voice.

"Like this one?"

"Yes."

"This makes the ninth."

Mrs. Babcock scrutinized the floor. It was almost covered with braided rugs, and they were all alike.

"I declare I don't see where you'll put another in here," said she.

"I guess I can lay 'em a little thicker over there by the what-not."

"Well, mebbe you can; but I declare I shouldn't scarcely think you needed another. I shouldn't think your carpet would wear out till the day of judgment. What made you have them mats all jest alike?"

"I like 'em better so," replied Amanda, with dignity.

"Well, of course, if you do there ain't nothin' to say; it's your carpet an' your mats," returned Mrs. Babcock, with grim apology.

There were two curious features about Amanda Pratt's parlor: one was a gentle monotony of details; the other, a certain savor of the sea. It was like holding a shell to one's ear to enter Amanda's parlor. There was a faint suggestion of far-away sandy beaches, the breaking of waves, and the rush of salt winds. In the centre of the mantel-shelf stood a stuffed sea-gull; on either side shells were banked. The fire-place was flanked by great branches of coral, and on the top of the air-tight stove there stood always in summer-time, when there was no fire, a superb nautilus shell, like a little pearl vessel. The corner what-not, too, had its shelves heaped with shells and coral and choice bits of rainbow lava from vol-canic islands. Between the windows, instead of the conventional mahogany cardtable, stood one of Indian lacquer, and on it was a little inlaid cabinet that was brought from over seas. The whole room in this little inland cottage, far beyond the salt fragrance of the sea, seemed like one of those marine fossils sometimes found miles from the coast. It indicated the presence of the sea in the lives of Amanda's race. Her grandfather had been a seafaring man, and so had her father, until late in life, when he had married an inland woman, and settled down among waves of timothy and clover on her paternal acres.

Amanda was like her mother, she had nothing of the sea tastes in her nature. She was full of loyal conservatism toward the marine ornaments of her parlor, but she secretly preferred her own braided rugs, and the popular village fancy-work, in which she was quite skilful. On each of her chairs was a tidy, and the tidies were all alike; in the corners of the room were lambrequins, all worked after the same pattern in red worsted and beads. On one wall hung a group of pictures framed in cardboard, four little colored prints of crosses twined with flowers, and they were all alike. "Why didn't you get them crosses different?" many a neighbor had said to her — these crosses, with some variation of the entwining foliage, had been very popular in the rural neighborhood — and Amanda had replied with quick dignity that she liked them better the way she had them. Amanda maintained the monotony of her life as fiercely as her fathers had pursued the sea. She was like a little animal born with a rebound to its own track, from whence no amount of pushing could keep it long.

Mrs. Babcock glanced sharply around the room as she sewed; she was anxious to divert Amanda's mind from the mats. "Don't the moths ever git into that stuffed bird over there?" she asked suddenly, indicating the gull on the shelf with a side-wise jerk of her head.

"No; I ain't never had a mite of trouble with 'em," replied Amanda. "I always keep a little piece of camphor tucked under his wing feathers."

"Well, you're lucky. Mis' Jackson she had a stuffed canary-bird all eat up with 'em. She had to put him in the stove; couldn't do nothin' with him. She felt real bad about it. She'd thought a good deal of the bird when he was alive, an' he was stuffed real handsome, an' settin' on a little green sprig. She use to keep him on her parlor shelf; he was jest the right size. It's a pity your bird is quite so big, ain't it?"

"I s'pose he's jest the way he was made," returned Amanda shortly.

"Of course he is. I ain't findin' no fault with him; all is, I thought he was kind of big for the shelf; but then birds do perch on dreadful little places." Mrs. Babcock, full of persistency in exposing herself to rebuffs, was very sensitive and easily cowed by one. "Let me see — he's quite old. Your grandfather bought him, didn't he?" said she, in a mollifying tone.

Amanda nodded. "He's a good deal older than I am," said she.

"It's queer how some things that ain't of no account really in the world last, while others that's worth so much more don't," Mrs. Babcock remarked, meditatively. "Now, there's that bird there, lookin' jest as nice and handsome, and there's the one that bought him and brought him home, in his grave out of sight."

"There's a good many queer things in this world," rejoined Amanda, with a sigh.

"I guess there is," said Mrs. Babcock. "Now you can jest look round this room, an' see all the things that belonged to your folks that's dead an' gone, and it seems almost as if they was immortal instead of them. An' it's goin' to be jest the same way with us; the clothes that's hangin' up in our closets are goin' to outlast us. Well, there's one thing about it — this world ain't *our* abidin'-place."

Mrs. Babcock shook her head resolutely, and began to fold up her work. She rolled the unbleached cloth into a hard smooth bundle, with the scissors, thimble, and thread inside, and the needle quilted in.

"You ain't goin'?" said Amanda.

"Yes, I guess I must. I've got to be home by half-past five to get supper, an' I thought I'd jest look in at Mis' Field's a minute. Do you s'pose she's to home?"

"I shouldn't wonder if she was. I ain't seen her go out anywhere."

"Well, I dun'no' when I've been in there, an' I dun'no' but she'd think it was kinder queer if I went right into the house and didn't go near her."

Amanda arose, letting the mat slide to the floor, and went into the bedroom to get Mrs. Babcock's bonnet and light shawl.

"I wish you wouldn't be in such a hurry," said she, using the village formula of hospitality to a departing guest.

"It don't seem to me I've been in much of a hurry. I've stayed here the whole afternoon."

Suddenly Mrs. Babcock, pinning on her shawl, thrust her face close to Amanda's. "I want to know if it's true Lois Field is so miserable?" she whispered.

"Well, I dun'no'. She don't look jest right, but she an' her mother won't own up but what she's well."

"Goin' the way Mis' Maxwell did, ain't she?"

"I dun'no'. I'm worried about her myself — dreadful worried. Lois is a nice girl as ever was."

"She ain't give up her school?"

Amanda shook her head.

"I shouldn't think her mother'd have her."

"I s'pose she feels as if she'd got to." Mrs. Babcock dropped her voice still lower. "They're real poor, ain't they?"

"I guess they ain't got much."

"I s'pose they hadn't. Well, I hope Lois ain't goin' down. I heard she looked dreadful. Mis' Jackson she was in yesterday, talkin' about it. Well, you come over an' see me, Mandy. Bring your sewin' over some afternoon."

"Well, mebbe I will. I don't go out a great deal, you know."

The two women grimaced to each other in a friendly fashion, then Amanda shut her door, and Mrs. Babcock pattered softly and heavily across the little entry, and opened Mrs. Field's door. She pressed the old brass latch with a slight show of ceremonious hesitancy, but she never thought of knocking. There was no one in the room, which had a clean and sparse air. The chairs all stood back against the walls, and left in the centre a wide extent of faded carpet, full of shadowy gray scrolls.

Mrs. Babcock stood for a moment staring in and listening.

There was a faint sound of a voice seemingly from a room beyond. She called, softly, "Mis' Field!" There was no response. She advanced then resolutely over the stretch of carpet toward the bedroom door. She opened it, then gave a little embarrassed grunt, and began backing away.

Mrs. Field was in there, kneeling beside the bed, praying. She started and looked up at Mrs. Babcock with a kind of solemn abashedness, her long face flushed. Then she got up. "Good-afternoon," said she.

"Good-afternoon," returned Mrs. Babcock. She tried to smile and recover her equanimity. "I've been into Mandy Pratt's," she went on, "an' I thought I'd jest look in here a minute before I went home, but I wouldn't have come in so if I'd known you was — busy."

"Come out in the other room an' sit down," said Mrs. Field.

Mrs. Babcock's agitated bulk followed her over the gray carpet, and settled into the rocking-chair at one of the front windows. Mrs. Field seated herself at the other.

"It's been a pleasant day, ain't it?" said she.

"Real pleasant. I told Mr. Babcock this noon that I was goin' to git out somewheres this afternoon come what would. I've been cooped up all the spring house-cleanin', an' now I'm goin' to git out. I dun'no' when I've been anywhere. I ain't been into Mandy's sence Christmas that I know of — I ain't been in to set down, anyway; an' I've been meanin' to run in an' see you all winter, Mis' Field." All the trace of confusion now left in Mrs. Babcock's manner was a weak volubility.

"It's about all anybody can do to do their housework, if they do it thorough," returned Mrs. Field. "I s'pose you've been takin' up carpets?"

"Took up every carpet in the house. I do every year. Some folks don't, but I can't stand it. I'm afraid of moths, too. I s'pose you've got your cleanin' all done?"

"Yes, I've got it about done."

"Well, I shouldn't think you could do so much, Mis' Field, with your hands."

Mrs. Field's hands lay in her lap, yellow and heavily corrugated, the finger-joints in great knots, which looked as if they had been tied in the bone. Mrs. Babcock eyed them pitilessly.

"How are they now?" she inquired. "Seems to me they look worse than they used to."

Mrs. Field regarded her hands with a staid, melancholy air. "Well, I dun'no'."

"Seems to me they look worse. How's Lois, Mis' Field?"

"She's pretty well, I guess. I dun'no' why she ain't."

"Somebody was sayin' the other day that she looked dreadfully."

Mrs. Field had heretofore held herself with a certain slow dignity. Now her manner suddenly changed, and she spoke fast. "I dun'no' what folks mean talkin' so," said she. "Lois ain't been lookin' very well, as I know of, lately; but it's the spring of the year, an' she's always apt to feel it."

"Mebbe that is it," replied the other, with a doubtful inflection. "Let's see, you called it consumption that ailed your sister, didn't you, Mis' Field?"

"I s'pose it was."

Mrs. Babcock stared with cool reflection at the other woman's long, pale face, with its high cheek-bones and deep-set eyes and wide, drooping mouth. She was deliberating whether or not to ask for some information that she wanted. "Speakin' of your sister," said she finally, with a casual air, "her husband's father is livin', ain't he?"

"He was the last I knew."

"I s'pose he's worth considerable property?"

"Yes, I s'pose he is."

"Well, I want to know. Somebody was speakin' about it the other day, an' they said they thought he did, an' I told 'em I didn't believe it. He never helped your sister's husband any, did he?"

Mrs. Field did not reply for a moment. Mrs. Babcock was leaning forward and smiling ingratiatingly, with keen eyes upon her face.

"I dun'no' as he did. But I guess Edward never expected he would much," said she.

"Well, I told 'em I didn't believe he did. I declare! it seemed pretty tough, didn't it?"

"I dun'no'. I thought of it some along there when Edward was sick."

"I declare, I should have thought you'd wrote to him about it."

Mrs. Field said nothing.

"Didn't you ever?" Mrs. Babcock asked.

"Well, yes; I wrote once when he was first taken sick."

"An' he didn't take any notice of it?"

Mrs. Field shook her head.

"He's a regular old skinflint, ain't he?" said Mrs. Babcock.

"I guess he's a pretty set kind of a man."

"Set! I should call it more'n set. Now, Mis' Field, I'd really like to know something. I ain't curious, but I've heard so many stories about it that I'd really like to know the truth of it once. Somebody was speakin' about it the other day, an' it don't seem right for stories to be goin' the rounds when there ain't no truth in 'em. Mis' Field, what was it set Edward Maxwell's father agin' him?" Mrs. Babcock's voice sank to a whisper, she leaned farther forward, and gazed at Mrs. Field with crafty sweetness.

Mrs. Field looked out of the window.

"Well, I s'pose it was some trouble about money matters."

"Money matters?"

"Yes, I s'pose so."

"Mis' Field, *what* did he do?"

Mrs. Field did not reply. She looked out of the window at the green banks in front. Her face was inscrutable.

Mrs. Babcock drew herself up. "Course I don't want you to tell me nothin' you don't want to," said she, with injured dignity. "I ain't pryin' into things that folks don't want me to know about; it wa'n't never my way. All is, I thought I'd like to know the truth of it, whether there was anything in them stories or not."

"Oh, I'd jest as soon tell you," rejoined Mrs. Field quietly. "I was jest a-thinkin'. As near as I can tell you, Mis' Babcock, Edward's father he let him have some money, and Edward he speculated with it on something contrary to his advice, an' lost it, an' that made the trouble."

"Was that all?" asked Mrs. Babcock, with a disappointed air.

"Yes, I s'pose it was."

"I want to know!" Mrs. Babcock leaned back with a sigh. "Well, there's another thing," she said presently. "Somebody was sayin' the other day that you thought Esther caught the consumption from her husband. I wanted to know if you did."

Mrs. Field's face twitched. "Well," she replied, "I dun'no'. I've heard consumption was catchin', an' she was right over him the whole time."

"Well, I don't know. I ain't never been able to take much stock in catchin' consumption. There was Mis' Gay night an' day with Susan for ten years, an' she's jest as well as anybody. I should be afraid 'twas a good deal likelier to be in your family. Does Lois cough?"

"None to speak of."

"Well, there's more kinds of consumption than one."

Mrs. Babcock made quite a long call. She shook Mrs. Field's hand warmly at parting. "I want to know, does Lois like honey?" said she.

"Yes, she's real fond of it."

"Well, I'm goin' to send her over a dish of it. Ours was uncommon nice this year. It's real good for a cough."

On her way home Mrs. Babcock met Lois Field coming from school attended by a little flock of children. Mrs. Babcock stopped, and looked sharply at her small, delicately pretty face, with its pointed chin and deep-set blue eyes.

"How are you feelin' to-night, Lois?" she inquired, in a tone of forcible commiseration.

"I'm pretty well, thank you," said Lois.

"Seems to me you're lookin' pretty slim. You'd ought to take a little vacation." Mrs. Babcock surveyed her with a kind of pugnacious pity.

Lois stood quite erect in the midst of the children. "I don't think I need any vacation," said she, smiling constrainedly. She pushed gently past Mrs. Babcock, with the children at her heels.

"You'd better take a little one," Mrs. Babcock called after her.

Lois kept on as if she did not hear. Her face was flushed, and her head seemed full of beating pulses.

One of the children, a thin little girl in a blue dress, turned around and grimaced at Mrs. Babcock; another pulled Lois' dress. "Teacher, Jenny Whitcomb is makin' faces at Mis' Babcock," she drawled.

"Jenny!" said Lois sharply; and the little girl turned her face with a scared nervous giggle. "You mustn't ever do such a thing as that again," said Lois. She reached down and took the child's little restive hand and led her along.

Lois had not much farther to go. The children all clamored, "Good-by, teacher!" when she turned in at her own gate.

She went in through the sitting-room to the kitchen, and settled down into a chair with her hat on.

"Well, so you've got home," said her mother; she was moving about preparing supper. She smiled anxiously at Lois as she spoke.

Lois smiled faintly, but her forehead was frowning. "Has that

Mrs. Babcock been here?" she asked.

"Yes. Did you meet her?"

"Yes, I did; and I'd like to know what she meant telling me I'd ought to take a vacation, and I looked bad. I wish people would let me alone tellin' me how I look."

"She meant well, I guess," said her mother, soothingly. "She said she was goin' to send you over a dish of her honey."

"I don't want any of her honey. I don't see what folks want to send things in to me, as if I were sick, for."

"Oh, I guess she thought I'd like some too," returned her mother, with a kind of stiff playfulness. "You needn't think you're goin' to have all that honey."

"I don't want any of it," said Lois. The window beside which she sat was open; under it, in the back yard, was a little thicket of mint, and some long sprays of sweetbrier bowing over it. Lois reached out and broke off a piece of the sweetbrier and smelled it.

"Supper's ready," said her mother, presently; and she took off her hat and went listlessly over to the table.

The table, covered with a white cloth, was set back against the wall, with only one leaf spread. There were bread and butter and custards and a small glass dish of rhubarb sauce for supper.

Lois looked at the dish. "I didn't know the rhubarb was grown," said she.

"I managed to get enough for supper," replied her mother, in a casual voice.

Nobody would have dreamed how day after day she had journeyed stiffly down to the old garden spot behind the house to watch the progress of the rhubarb, and how triumphantly she had brought up those green and rosy stalks. Lois had always been very fond of rhubarb.

She ate it now with a keen relish. Her mother contrived that she should have nearly all of it; she made a show of helping herself twice, but she took very little. But it was to her as if she also tasted every spoonful which her daughter ate, and as if it had the flavor of a fruit of Paradise and satisfied her very soul.

After supper Lois began packing up the cups and saucers.

"Now you go in the other room an' set down, an' let me take care of the dishes," said Mrs. Field, timidly.

Lois faced about instantly. "Now, mother, I'd just like to know what you mean?" said she. "I guess I ain't quite so far gone but what I can wash up a few dishes. You act as if you wanted to make me out sick in spite of myself."

"I thought mebbe you was kind of tired," said her mother,

apologetically.

"I ain't tired. I'm jest as well able to wash up the supper dishes as I ever was." Lois carried the cups and saucers to the sink with a resolute air, and Mrs. Field said no more. She went into her bedroom to change her dress; she was going to evening meeting.

Lois washed and put away the dishes; then she went into the sitting-room, and sat down by the open window. She leaned her cheek against the chairback and looked out; a sweet almond fragrance of cherry and apple blossoms came into her face; over across the fields a bird was calling. Lois did not think it tangibly, but it was to her as if the blossom scent and the bird call came out of her own future. She was ill, poor, and overworked, but she was not unhappy, for her future was yet, in a way, untouched; she had not learned to judge of it by hard precedent, nor had any mistake of hers made a miserable certainty of it. It still looked to her as fair ahead as an untrodden field of heaven.

She was quite happy as she sat there; but when her mother, in her black woollen dress, entered, she felt instantly nervous and fretted. Mrs. Field said nothing, but the volume and impetus of her anxiety when she saw her daughter's head in the window seemed to actually misplace the air.

Presently she went to the window, and leaned over to shut it.

"Don't shut the window, mother," said Lois.

"I'm dreadful afraid you'll catch cold, child."

"No, I sha'n't, either. I wish you wouldn't fuss so, mother."

Mrs. Field stood back; the meeting bell began to ring.

"Goin' to meetin', mother?" Lois asked, in a pleasanter voice.

"I thought mebbe I would."

"I guess I won't go. I want to sew some on my dress this evenin'."

"Sha'n't you mind stayin' alone, if I go?"

"Mind stayin' alone? of course I sha'n't. You get the strangest ideas lately, mother."

Mrs. Field put on her black bonnet and shawl, and started. The bell tolled, and she passed down the village street with a stiff steadiness of gait. She felt eager to go to meeting to-night. This old New England woman, all of whose traditions were purely orthodox, was all unknowingly a fetich-worshipper in a time of trouble. Ever since her daughter had been ill, she had had a terrified impulse in her meeting-going. It seemed to her that if she stayed away, Lois might be worse. Unconsciously her church attendance became a species of spell, or propitiation to a terrifying deity, and the wild instinct of the African awoke in the New

England woman.

When she reached the church the bell had stopped ringing, and the vestry windows were parallelograms of yellow light; the meeting was in the vestry.

Mrs. Field entered, and took a seat well toward the front. The room was half filled with people, and the mass of them were elderly and middle-aged women. There were rows of their homely, faded, and strong-lined faces set in sober bonnets, a sprinkling of solemn old men, a few bright-ribboned girls, and in the background a settee or two of smart young fellows. Right in front of Mrs. Field sat a pretty girl with roses in her hat. She was about Lois' age, and had been to school with her.

Mrs. Field, erect and gaunt, with a look of goodness so settled and pre-eminent in her face that it had almost the effect of a smile, sat and listened to the minister. He was a young man with boyish shoulders, and a round face, which he screwed nervously as he talked. He was vehement, and strung to wiriness with new enthusiasm; he seemed to toss the doctrines like footballs back and forth before the eyes of the people.

Mrs. Field listened intently, but all the time it was as if she were shut up in a corner with her own God and her own religion. There are as many side chapels as there are individual sorrows in every church.

After the minister finished his discourse, the old men muttered prayers, with long pauses between. Now and then a young woman played a gospel tune on a melodeon, and a woman in the same seat with Mrs. Field led the singing. She was past middle age, but her voice was still sweet, although once in a while it quavered. She had sung in the church choir ever since she was a child, and was the prima donna of the village. The young girl with roses in her hat who sat in front of Mrs. Field also sang with fervor, although her voice was little more than a sweetly husky breath. She kept her eyes, at once bold and timid, fixed upon the young minister as she sang.

When meeting was done, and Mrs. Field arose, the girl spoke to her. She had a pretty blush on her round cheeks, and she smiled at Mrs. Field in the same way that she would soon smile at the young minister.

"How's Lois to-night, Mrs. Field?" said she.

"She's pretty well, thank you, Ida."

"I heard she was sick."

"Oh, no, she ain't sick. The spring weather has made her feel kind of tired out, that's all. It 'most always does."

"Well, I'm glad she isn't sick," said the girl, her radiant absent eyes turned upon the minister, who was talking with some one at the desk. "She wasn't out to meeting, and I didn't know but she might be."

"She thought she wouldn't —" began Mrs. Field, but the girl was gone. The minister had started down the other aisle, and she met him at the door.

Several other people inquired for Lois as Mrs. Field made her way out; some had heard she was ill in bed. She had an errand to do at the store on her way home; when she reached it she went in, and stood waiting at the counter.

There were a number of men lounging about the large, rank, becluttered room, and there were several customers. The village post-office was in one corner of the store. There were only two clerks besides the proprietor, who was postmaster as well. Mrs. Field had to wait quite a while; but at last she had made her purchases, and was just stepping out the door, when a voice arrested her. "Mis' Field," it said.

She turned, and saw the postmaster coming toward her with a letter in his hand. The lounging men twisted about and stared lazily. The postmaster was a short, elderly man with shelving gray whiskers, and a wide, smiling mouth, which he was drawing down solemnly.

"Mis' Field, here's a letter I want you to look at; it come this mornin'," he said, in a low voice.

Mrs. Field took the letter. It was directed, in a fair round hand, to Mrs. Esther Maxwell; that had been her dead sister's name. She stood looking at it, her face drooping severely. "It was sent to my sister," said she.

"I s'posed so. Well, I thought I'd hand it to you."

Mrs. Field nodded gravely, and put the letter in her pocket. She was again passing out, when somebody nudged her heavily. It was Mrs. Green, a woman who lived in the next house beyond hers.

"Jest wait a minute," she said, "an' I'll go along with you."

So Mrs. Field stood back and waited, while her neighbor pushed forward to the counter. After a little she drew the letter from her pocket and studied the superscription. The post-mark was Elliot. She supposed the letter to be from her dead sister's father-in-law, who lived there.

"I may jest as well open it an' see what it is while I'm waitin'," she thought.

She tore open the envelope slowly and clumsily with her stiff fingers, and held up the letter so the light struck it. She could not read strange writing easily, and this was a nearly illegible scrawl. However, after the first few words, she seemed to absorb it by some higher faculty than reading. In a short time she had the gist of the letter. It was from a lawyer who signed himself Daniel Tuxbury. He stated formally that Thomas Maxwell was dead; that he had left a will greatly to Esther Maxwell's advantage, and that it would be advisable for her to come to Elliot at an early date if possible. Inclosed was a copy of the will. It was dated several years ago. All Thomas Maxwell's property was bequeathed without reserve to his son's widow, Esther Maxwell, should she survive him. In case of her decease before his own, the whole was to revert to his brother's daughter, Flora Maxwell.

Jane Field read the letter through twice, then she folded it, replaced it in the envelope, and stood erect by the store door. She could see Mrs. Green's broad shawled back among the customers at the calico counter. Once in a while she looked around with a beseeching and apologetic smile.

Mrs. Field thought, "I won't say a word to her about it." However, she was conscious of no evil motive; it was simply because she was naturally secretive. She looked pale and rigid.

Mrs. Green remarked it when she finally approached with her parcel of calico.

"Why, what's the matter, Mis' Field?" she exclaimed. "You ain't sick, be you?"

"No. Why?"

"Seems to me you look dreadful pale. It was too bad to keep you standin' there so long, but I couldn't get waited on before. I think Mr. Robbins had ought to have more help. It's too much for him with only two clerks, an' the post-office to tend, too. I see you got a letter." Mrs. Field nodded. The two women went down the steps into the street.

"How's Lois to-night?" Mrs. Green asked as they went along.

"I guess she's about as usual. She didn't say but what she was."

"She ain't left off her school, has she?"

"No," replied Mrs. Field, stiffly, "she ain't."

Suddenly Mrs. Green stopped and laid a heavy hand on Mrs. Field's arm. "Look here, Mis' Field, I dun'no' as you'll thank me for it, but I'm goin' to speak real plain to you, the way I'd thank anybody to if 'twas my Jenny. I'm dreadful afraid you don't realize how bad Lois is, Mis' Field."

"Mebbe I don't." Mrs. Field's voice sounded hard.

The other woman looked perplexedly at her for a moment,

then she went on:

"Well, if you do, mebbe I hadn't ought to said anything; but I was dreadful afraid you didn't, an' then when you come to, perhaps when 'twas too late, you'd never forgive yourself. She hadn't ought to teach school another day, Mis' Field."

"I dun'no how it's goin' to be helped," Mrs. Field said again, in her hard voice.

"Mis' Field, I know it ain't any of my business, an' I don't know but you'll think I'm interferin'; but I can't help it nohow when I think of — my Abby, an' how — she went down. *Ain't* you got anybody that could help you a little while till she gets better an' able to work?"

"I dun'no' of anybody."

"Wouldn't your sister's husband's father? Ain't he got considerable property?"

Mrs. Field turned suddenly, her voice sharpened, "I've asked him all I'm ever goin' to — there! I let Esther's husband have fifteen hundred dollars that my poor husband saved out of his hard earnin's, an' he lost it in his business; an' after he died I wrote to his father, an' I told him about it. I thought mebbe he'd be willin' to be fair, an' pay his son's debts, if he didn't have much feelin'. There was Esther an' Lois an' me, an' not a cent to live on, an' Esther she was beginnin' to be feeble. But he jest sent me back my letter, an' he'd wrote on the back of it that he wa'n't responsible for any of his son's debts. I said then I'd never go to him agin, and I didn't; an' Esther didn't when she was sick an' dyin'; an' I never let him know when she died, an' I don't s'pose he knows she is dead to this day."

"Oh, Mis' Field, you didn't have to lose all that money!"

"Yes, I did, every dollar of it."

"I declare it's wicked."

"There's a good many things that's wicked, an' sometimes I think some things ain't wicked that we've always thought was. I don't know but the Lord meant everybody to have what belonged to them in spite of everything."

Mrs. Green stared. "I guess I don't know jest what you mean, Mis' Field."

"I meant everybody ought to have what's their just due, an' I believe the Lord will uphold them in it. I've about come to the conclusion that folks ought to lay hold of justice themselves if there ain't no other way, an' that's what we've got hands for." Suddenly Mrs. Field's manner changed. "I know Lois hadn't ought to be teachin' school as well as you do," said she. "I ain't said much about it, it ain't my way, but I've known it all the time."

"She'd ought to take a vacation, Mis' Field, an' get away from here for a spell. Folks say Green River ain't very healthy. They say these low meadow-lands are bad. I worried enough about it after my Abby died, thinkin' what might have been done. It does seem to me that if something was done right away, Lois might get up; but there ain't no use waitin'. I've seen young girls go down; it seems sometimes as if there wa'n't nothin' more to them than flowers, an' they fade away in a day. I've been all through it. Mis' Field, you don't mind my speakin' so, do you? Oh, Mis' Field, don't feel so bad! I'm real sorry I said anythin'."

Mrs. Field was shaking with great sobs. "I ain't — blamin' you," she said, brokenly.

Mrs. Green got out her own handkerchief. "Mis' Field, I wouldn't have spoken a word, but — I felt as if something ought to be done, if there could be; an' — I thought — so much about my — poor Abby. Lois always makes me think of her; she's jest about her build; an' — I didn't know as you — realized."

"I realized enough," returned Mrs. Field, catching her breath as she walked on.

"Now I hope you don't feel any worse because I spoke as I did," Mrs. Green said, when they reached the gate of the Pratt house.

"You ain't told me anything I didn't know," replied Mrs. Field.

Mrs. Green felt for one of her distorted hands; she held it a second, then she dropped it. Mrs. Field let it hang stiffly the while. It was a fervent demonstration to them, the evidence of unwonted excitement and the deepest feeling. When Mrs. Field entered her sitting-room, the first object that met her eyes was Lois' face. She was tilted back in the rocking-chair, her slender throat was exposed, her lips were slightly parted, and there was a glassy gleam between her half-open eyelids. Her mother stood looking at her.

Suddenly Lois opened her eyes wide and sat up. "What are you standing there looking at me so for, mother?" she said, in her weak, peevish voice.

"I ain't lookin' at you, child. I've jest come home from meetin'. I guess you've been asleep."

"I haven't been asleep a minute. I heard you open the outside door."

Mrs. Field's hand verged toward the letter in her pocket. Then she began untying her bonnet.

Lois arose, and lighted another lamp. "Well, I guess I'll go to bed," said she.

"Wait a minute," her mother returned.

Lois paused inquiringly.

"Never mind," her mother said, hastily. "You needn't stop. I can tell you jest as well to-morrow."

"What was it?"

"Nothin' of any account. Run along."

CHAPTER II

The next morning Lois had gone to her school and her mother had not yet shown the letter to her. She went about as usual, doing her housework slowly and vigorously. Mrs. Field's cleanliness was proverbial in this cleanly New England neighborhood. It almost amounted to asceticism; her rooms, when her work was finished, had the bareness and purity of a nun's cell. There was never any bloom of dust on Mrs. Field's furniture; there was only the hard, dull glitter of the wood. Her few chairs and tables looked as if waxed; the paint was polished in places from her doors and window-casings; her window-glass gave out green lights like jewels; and all this she did with infinite pains and slowness, as there was hardly a natural movement left in her rheumatic hands. But there was in her nature an element of stern activity that must have its outcome in some direction, and it took the one that it could find. Jane had used to take in sewing before her hands were diseased. In her youth she had learned the trade of a tailoress; when ready-made clothing, even for children, came into use, she made dresses. Her dresses had been long-waisted and stiffly boned, with high, straight biases, seemingly fitted to her own nature instead of her customers' forms; but they had been strongly and faithfully sewed, and her stitches held fast as the rivets on a coat of mail. Now she could not sew. She could knit, and that was all, besides her housework, that she could do.

This morning, while dusting a little triangular what-not that stood in a corner of her sitting-room, she came across a small box that held some old photographs. The box was made of a kind of stucco-work — shells held in place by a bed of putty. Amanda Pratt had made it and given it to her. Mrs. Field took up this box and dusted it carefully; then she opened it, and took out the photographs one by one.

After a while she stopped; she did not take out any more, but she looked intently at one; then she replaced all but that one, got painfully up from the low foot-stool where she had been sitting, and went out of her room across the entry to Amanda's, with the photograph in her hand.

Amanda sat at her usual window, sewing on her rug. The sunlight came in, and her shadow, set in a bright square, wavered on the floor; the clock out in the kitchen ticked. Amanda looked up when Mrs. Field entered. "Oh, it's you?" said she. "I wondered who was comin'. Set down, won't you?"

Mrs. Field went over to Amanda and held out the photograph. "I want to see if you can tell me who this is."

Amanda took the photograph and held it toward the light. She compressed her lips and wrinkled her forehead. "Why, it's you, of course — ain't it?"

Mrs. Field made no reply; she stood looking at her.

"Why, ain't it you?" Amanda asked, looking from the picture to her in a bewildered way.

"No; it's Esther."

"Esther?"

"Yes, it's Esther."

"Well, I declare! When was it took?"

"About ten years ago, when she was in Elliot."

"Well, all I've got to say is, if anybody had asked me, I'd have said it was took for you yesterday. Why, Mis' Field, what's the matter?"

"There ain't anything the matter."

"Why, you look dreadfully."

Mrs. Field's face was pale, and there was a curious look about her whole figure. It seemed as if shrinking from something, twisting itself rigidly, as a fossil tree might shrink in a wind that could move it.

"I feel well 'nough," said she. "I guess it's the light."

"Well, mebbe 'tis," replied Amanda, still looking anxiously at her. "Of course you know if you feel well, but you do look dreadful white to me. Don't you want some water, or a swaller of cold tea?"

"No, I don't want a single thing; I'm well enough." Mrs. Field's tone was almost surly. She held out her hand for the photograph. "I must be goin'," she continued; "I ain't got my dustin' done. I jest come across this, an' I thought I'd show it to you, an' see what you said."

"Well, I shouldn't have dreamed but what it was yours; but then you an' your sister did look jest alike. I never could tell you apart when you first came here."

"Folks always said we looked alike. We always used to be took for each other when we was girls, an' I think we looked full as much alike after our hair begun to turn. Mine was a little lighter than hers, an' that made some difference betwixt us before. It didn't show when we was both gray."

"I shouldn't have thought 'twould. Well, I must say, I shouldn't dream but what that picture was meant for you."

Mrs. Field took her way out of the room.

"How's Lois this mornin'?" Amanda called after her.

"About the same, I guess."

"I saw her goin' out of the yard this mornin', an' I thought she walked dreadful weak."

"I guess she don't walk any too strong."

When Mrs. Field was in her own room she stowed away the photograph in the shell box; then she got a little broom and brushed the shell-work carefully; she thought it looked dusty in spite of her rubbing.

When the dusting was done it was time for her to get her dinner ready. Indeed, there was not much leisure for Mrs. Field all day. She seldom sat down for long at a time. From morning until night she kept up her stiff resolute march about her house.

At half-past twelve she had the dinner on the table, but Lois did not come. Her mother went into the sitting-room, sat down beside a window, and watched. The town clock struck one. Mrs. Field went outdoors and stood by the front gate, looking down the road. She saw a girl coming in the distance with a flutter of light skirts, and she exclaimed with gladness, "There she is!" The girl drew nearer, and she saw it was Ida Starr in a dress that looked like Lois'.

The girl stopped when she saw Mrs. Field at the gate. "Good-morning," said she.

"Good-mornin', Ida."

"It's a beautiful day."

Mrs. Field did not reply; she gazed past her down the road, her face all one pale frown.

The girl looked curiously at her. "I hope Lois is pretty well this morning?" she said, in her amiable voice.

Mrs. Field responded with a harsh outburst that fairly made her start back.

"No," she cried out, "she ain't well; she's sick. She wa'n't fit to go to school. She couldn't hardly crawl out of the yard. She ain't got home, an' I'm terrible worried. I dun'no' but she's fell down."

"Maybe she just thought she wouldn't come home."

"No; that ain't it. She never did such a thing as that without saying something about it; she'd know I'd worry."

Mrs. Field craned her neck farther over the gate, and peered down the road. Beside the gate stood two tall bushes, all white with flowers that grew in long white racemes, and they framed her distressed face.

"Look here, Mrs. Field," said the girl, "I'll tell you what I'll do. The school-house isn't much beyond my house; I'll just run over there and see if there's anything the matter; then I'll come back right off, and let you know."

"Oh, will you?"

"Of course I will. Now don't you worry, Mrs. Field; I don't believe it's anything."

The girl nodded back at her with her pretty smile; then she sped away with a light tilting motion. Mrs. Field stood a few minutes longer, then she went up the steps into the house. She opened Amanda Pratt's door instead of her own, and went through the sitting-room to the kitchen, from whence she could hear the clink of dishes.

"Lois ain't got home yet," said she, standing in the doorway.

Amanda set down the dish she was wiping. "Mis' Field, what do you mean?"

"What I say."

"Ain't she got home yet?"

"No, she ain't."

"Why, it's half-past one o'clock! She ain't comin'; it's time for school to begin. Look here, Mis' Field, I guess she felt kind of tired, an' thought she wouldn't come."

Mrs. Field shook her head with a sort of remorselessness toward all comfort. "She's fell down."

"Oh, Mis' Field! you don't s'pose so?"

"The Starr girl's gone to find out."

Mrs. Field turned to go.

"Hadn't you better stay here till she comes?" asked Amanda, anxiously.

"No; I must go home." Suddenly Mrs. Field looked fiercely around. "I'll tell you what 'tis, Mandy Pratt, an' you mark my words! I ain't goin' to stan' this kind of work much longer! I ain't goin' to see all the child I've got in the world murdered; for that's what it is — it's murder!"

Mrs. Field went through the sitting-room with a stiff rush, and Amanda followed her.

"Oh, Mis' Field, don't take on so — don't!" she kept saying.

Mrs. Field went through the house into her own kitchen. The little white-laid table stood against the wall; the tea-kettle steamed and rocked on the stove; the room was full of savory odors. Mrs. Field set the tea-kettle back where it would not boil so hard. These little household duties had become to her almost as involuntary as the tick of her own pulses. No matter what hours of agony they told off, the pulses ticked; and in every stress of life she would set the tea-kettle back if it were necessary. Amanda stood in the door, trembling. All at once there was a swift roll of wheels in the yard past the window. "Somebody's come!" gasped Amanda. Mrs.

Field rushed to the back door, and Amanda after her. There was a buggy drawn up close to the step, and a man was trying to lift Lois out.

Mrs. Field burst out in a great wail. "Oh, Lois! Lois! She's dead — she's dead!"

"No, she ain't dead," replied the man, in a drawling, jocular tone. "She's worth a dozen dead ones — ain't you, Lois? I found her layin' down side of the road kind of tuckered out, that's all, and I thought I'd give her a lift. Don't you be scared, Mis' Field. Now, Lois, you jest rest all your heft on me."

Lois' pale face and little reaching hands appeared around the wing of the buggy. Amanda ran around to the horse's head. He did not offer to start; but she stood there, and said, "Whoa, whoa," over and over, in a pleading, nervous voice. She was afraid to touch the bridle; she had a great terror of horses.

The man, who was Ida Starr's father, lifted Lois out, and carried her into the house. She struggled a little.

"I can walk," said she, in a weakly indignant voice.

Mr. Starr carried her into the sitting-room and laid her down on the sofa. She raised herself immediately, and sat up with a defiant air.

"Oh, dear child, do lay down," sobbed her mother.

She put her hand on Lois' shoulder and tried to force her gently backward, but the girl resisted.

"Don't, mother," said she. "I don't want to lie down."

Amanda had run into her own room for the camphor bottle. Now she leaned over Lois and put it to her nose. "Jest smell of this a little," she said. Lois pushed it away feebly.

"I guess Lois will have to take a little vacation," said Mr. Starr. "I guess I shall have to see about it, and let her have a little rest."

He was one of the school committee.

"I don't need any vacation," said Lois, in a peremptory tone.

"I guess we shall have to see about it," repeated Mr. Starr. There was an odd undertone of decision in his drawling voice. He was a large man, with a pleasant face full of double curves. "Good-day," said he, after a minute. "I guess I must be goin'."

"Good-day," said Lois. "I'm much obliged to you for bringing me home."

"You're welcome."

Amanda nodded politely when he withdrew, but Mrs. Field never looked at him. She stood with her eyes fixed upon Lois.

"What are you looking at me so for, mother?" said Lois, impatiently, turning her own face away.

Mrs. Field sank down on her knees before the sofa. "Oh, my child!" she wailed. "My child! my child!"

She threw her arms around the girl's slender waist, and clung to her convulsively. Lois cast a terrified glance up at Amanda.

"Does she think I ain't going to get well?" she asked, as if her mother were not present.

"Of course she don't," replied Amanda, with decision. She stooped and took hold of Mrs. Field's shoulders. "Now look here, Mis' Field," said she, "you ain't actin' like yourself. You're goin' to make Lois sick, if she ain't now, if you go on this way. You get up an' make her a cup of tea, an' get her somethin' to eat. Ten chances to one, that's all that ailed her. I don't believe she's eat enough to-day to keep a cat alive."

"I know all about it," moaned Mrs. Field. "It's jest what I expected. Oh, my child! my child! I have prayed an' done all I could, an' now it's come to this. I've got to give up. Oh, my child! my child!"

It was to this mother as though her daughter was not there, although she held her in her arms. She was in that abandon of grief which is the purest selfishness.

Amanda fairly pulled her to her feet. "Mis' Field, I'm ashamed of you!" said she, severely. "I should think you were beside yourself. Here's Lois better —"

"No, she ain't better. I know."

Mrs. Field straightened herself, and went out into the kitchen.

Lois looked again at Amanda, in a piteous, terrified fashion. "Oh," said she, "you don't think I'm so very sick, do you?"

"Very sick? No; of course you ain't. Your mother got dreadful nervous because you didn't come home. That's what made her act so. You look a good deal better than you did when you first came in."

"I feel better," said Lois. "I never saw mother act so in my life."

"She got all wrought up, waitin'. If I was you, I'd lay down a few minutes, jest on her account. I think it would make her feel easier."

"Well, I will, if you think I'd better; but there ain't a mite of need of it."

Lois laid her head down on the sofa arm.

"That's right," said Amanda. "You can jest lay there a little while. I'm goin' out to tell your mother to make you a cup of tea. That'll set you right up."

Amanda found Mrs. Field already making the tea. She measured it out carefully, and never looked around. Amanda stepped close to her.

"Mis' Field," she whispered, "I hope you wa'n't hurt by what I said. I meant it for the best."

"I sha'n't give way so again," said Mrs. Field. Her face had a curious determined expression.

"I hope you don't feel hurt?"

"No, I don't. I sha'n't give way so again." She poured the boiling water into the teapot, and set it on the stove.

Amanda looked at a covered dish on the stove hearth. "What was you goin' to have for dinner?" said she.

"Lamb broth. I'm goin' to heat up some for her. She didn't eat hardly a mouthful of breakfast."

"That's jest the thing for her. I'll get out the kettle and put it on to heat. I dun'no' of anything that gits cold any quicker than lamb broth, unless it's love."

Amanda put on a cheerful air as she helped Mrs. Field. Presently the two women carried in the little repast to Lois.

"She's asleep," whispered Amanda, who went first with the tea.

They stood looking at the young girl, stretched out her slender length, her white delicate profile showing against the black arm of the sofa.

Her mother caught her breath. "She's got to be waked up; she's got to have some nourishment, anyhow," said she. "Come, Lois, wake up, and have your dinner."

Lois opened her eyes. All the animation and defiance were gone from her face. She was so exhausted that she made no resistance to anything. She let them raise her, prop her up with a pillow, and nearly feed her with the dinner. Then she lay back, and her eyes closed.

Amanda went home, and Mrs. Field went back to the kitchen to put away the dinner dishes. She had eaten nothing herself, and now she poured some of the broth into a cup, and drank it down with great gulps without tasting it. It was simply filling of a necessity the lamp of life with oil.

After her housework was done, she sat down in the kitchen with her knitting. There was no sound from the other room.

The latter part of the afternoon Amanda came past the window and entered the back door. She carried a glass of foaming beer. Amanda was famous through the neighborhood for this beer, which she concocted from roots and herbs after an ancient recipe. It was pleasantly flavored with aromatic roots, and instinct with agreeable bitterness, being an innocently tonic old-maiden brew.

"I thought mebbe she'd like a glass of my beer," whispered Amanda. "I came round the house so's not to disturb her. How is she?"

"I guess she's asleep. I ain't heard a sound."

Amanda set the glass on the table. "Don't you think you'd ought to have a doctor, Mis' Field?" said she.

It seemed impossible that Lois could have heard, but her voice came shrilly from the other room: "No, I ain't going to have a doctor; there's no need of it. I sha'n't like it if you get one, mother."

"No, you sha'n't have one, dear child," her mother called back. "She was always jest so about havin' a doctor," she whispered to Amanda.

"I'll take in the beer if she's awake," said Amanda.

Lois looked up when she entered. "I don't want a doctor," said she, pitifully, rolling her blue eyes.

"Of course you sha'n't have a doctor if you don't want one," returned Amanda, soothingly. "I thought mebbe you'd like a glass of my beer."

Lois drank the beer eagerly, then she sank back and closed her eyes. "I'm going to get up in a minute, and sew on my dress," she murmured.

But she did not stir until her mother helped her to bed early in the evening.

The next day she seemed a little better. Luckily it was Saturday, so there was no worry about her school for her. She would not lie down, but sat in the rocking-chair with her needle-work in her lap. When any one came in, she took it up and sewed. Several of the neighbors had heard she was ill, and came to inquire. She told them, with a defiant air, that she was very well, and they looked shocked and nonplussed. Some of them beckoned her mother out into the entry when they took leave, and Lois heard them whispering together.

The next day, Sunday, Lois seemed about the same. She said once that she was going to church, but she did not speak of it again. Mrs. Field went. She suggested staying at home, but Lois was indignant.

"Stay at home with me, no sicker than I am! I should think you were crazy, mother," said she.

So Mrs. Field got out her Sunday clothes and went to meeting. As soon as she had gone, Lois coughed; she had been choking the cough back. She stood at the window, well back that people might not see her, and watched her mother pass down the street with her stiff glide. Mrs. Field's back and shoulders were rigidly steady when she walked; she might have carried a jar of water on her head without spilling it, like an Indian woman. Lois, small and slight although she was, walked like her mother. She held herself with the same resolute stateliness, when she could hold herself at all. The two women might, as far as their carriage went, have marched in a battalion with propriety.

Lois felt a certain relief when her mother had gone. Even when Mrs. Field made no expression of anxiety, there was a covert distress about her which seemed to enervate the atmosphere, and hinder the girl in the fight she was making against her own weakness. Lois had a feeling that if nobody would look at her nor speak about her illness, she could get well quickly of herself.

As for Mrs. Field, she was no longer eager to attend meeting; she went rather than annoy Lois. She was present at both the morning and afternoon services. They still had two services in Green River.

Jane Field, sitting in her place in church through the long sermons, had a mental experience that was wholly new to her. She looked at the white walls of the audience-room, the pulpit, the carpet, the pews. She noted the familiar faces of the people in their Sunday gear, the green light stealing through the long blinds, and all these accustomed sights gave her a sense of awful strangeness and separation. And this impression did not leave her when she was out on the street mingling with the homeward people; every greeting of an old neighbor strengthened it. She regarded the peaceful village houses with their yards full of new green grass and flowering bushes, and they seemed to have a receding dimness as she neared some awful shore. Even the click of her own gate as she opened it, the sound of her own feet on the path, the feel of the door-latch to her hand — all the little common belongings of her daily life were turned into so many stationary landmarks to prove her own retrogression and fill her with horror.

To-day, when people inquired for Lois, her mother no longer gave her customary replies. She said openly that her daughter was real miserable, and she was worried about her.

"I guess she's beginning to realize it," the women whispered to each other with a kind of pitying triumph. For there is a certain aggravation in our friends' not owning to even those facts which we deplore for them. It is provoking to have an object of pity balk. Mrs. Field's assumption that her daughter was not ill had half incensed her sympathizing neighbors; even Amanda had marvelled indignantly at it. But now the sudden change in her friend caused her to marvel still more. She felt a vague fear every time she thought of her. After Lois had gone to bed that Sunday night, her mother came into Amanda's room, and the two women sat together in the dusk. It was so warm that Amanda had set all the windows open, and the room was full of the hollow gurgling of the frogs — there was some low meadow-land behind the house.

"I want to know what you think of Lois?" said Mrs. Field, suddenly; her voice was high and harsh.

"Why, I don't know, hardly, Mis' Field."

"Well, I know. She's runnin' down. She won't ever be any better, unless I can do something. She's dyin' for the want of a little money, so she can stop work an' go away to some healthier place an' rest. She is; the Lord knows she is." Mrs. Field's voice was solemn, almost oratorical.

Amanda sat still; her long face looked pallid and quite unmoved in the low light; she was thinking what she could say.

But Mrs. Field went on; she was herself so excited to speech and action, the outward tendency of her own nature was so strong, that she failed to notice the course of another's. "She is," she repeated, argumentatively, as if Amanda had spoken, or she was acute enough to hear the voice behind silence; "there ain't any use talkin'."

There was a pause, a soft wind came into the room, the noise of the frogs grew louder, a whippoorwill called; it seemed as if the wide night were flowing in at the windows.

"What I want to know is," said Mrs. Field, "if you will take Lois in here to meals, an' look after her a week or two. Be you willin' to?"

"You ain't goin' away, Mis' Field?" There was a slow and contained surprise in Amanda's tone.

"Yes, I be; to-morrow mornin', if I live, on the early train. I be, if you're willin' to take Lois. I don't see how I can leave her any other way as she is now. You sha'n't be any loser by it, if you'll take her."

"Where be you goin', Mis' Field?"

"I don't want you to say anything about it. I don't want it all over town."

"I sha'n't say anything."

"Well, I'm goin' down to Elliot."

"You be?"

"Yes, I be. Old Mr. Maxwell's dead. I had a letter a night or two ago."

Amanda gasped, "He's dead?"

"Yes."

"What was the matter, do you know?"

"They called it paralysis. It was sudden."

Amanda hesitated. "I s'pose — you know anything about — his property?" said she.

"Yes; he left it all to my sister."

"Why, Mis' Field!"

"Yes; he left every cent of it to her."

"Oh, ain't it dreadful she's dead?"

"It's all been dreadful right along," said Mrs. Field.

"Of course," said Amanda, "I know she's better off than she'd be with all the money in the world; it ain't that; but it would do so much good to the livin'. Why, look here, Mis' Field, I dun'no' anything about law, but won't you have it if your sister's dead?"

"I'm goin' down there."

"It seems as if you'd ought to have somethin' anyway, after all you've done, lettin' his son have your money an' everything."

Amanda spoke with stern warmth. She had known about this grievance of her neighbor's for a long time.

"I'm goin' down there," repeated Mrs. Field.

"I would," said Amanda.

"I hate to leave Lois," said Mrs. Field; "but I don't see any other way."

"I'll take her," said Amanda, "if you're willin' to trust her with me."

"I've got to," replied Mrs. Field.

"Well, I'll do the best I can," replied Amanda.

She was considerably shaken. She felt her knees tremble. It was as if she were working a new tidy or rug pattern. Any variation of her peaceful monotony of existence jarred her whole nature like heavy wheels, and this was a startling one.

She wondered how Mrs. Field could bring herself to leave Lois. It seemed to her that she must have hopes of all the old man's property.

After Mrs. Field had gone home, and she, primly comfortable in her starched and ruffled dimities, lay on her high feather-bed between her smooth sheets, she settled it in her own mind that her neighbor would certainly have the property. She wondered if she and Lois would go to Elliot to live, and who would live in her tenement. The change was hard for her to contemplate, and she wept a little. Many a happiness comes to its object with outriders of sorrows to others.

Poor Amanda bemoaned herself over the changes that might come to her little home, and planned nervously her manner of living with Lois during the next week. Amanda had lived entirely alone for over twenty years; this admitting another to her own territory seemed as grave a matter to her as the admission of foreigners did to Japan. Indeed, all her kind were in a certain way foreigners to Amanda; and she was shy of them, she had so withdrawn herself by her solitary life, for solitariness is the farthest country of them all.

Amanda did not sleep much, and it was very early in the morning — she was standing before the kitchen looking-glass, twisting the rosettes of her front hair — when Mrs. Field came in to say good-by. Mrs. Field was gaunt and erect in her straight black clothes. She had her black veil tied over her bonnet to protect it from dust, and the black frame around her strong-featured face gave her a rigid, relentless look, like a female Jesuit. Lois came faltering behind her mother. She had a bewildered air, and she looked from her mother to Amanda with appealing significance, but she did not speak.

"Well, I've come to say good-by," said Mrs. Field.

Amanda had one side of her front hair between her lips while she twisted the other; she took it out. "Good-by, Mis' Field," she said. "I'll do the best I can for Lois. How soon do you s'pose you'll be back?"

"It's accordin' to how I get along. I've been tellin' Lois she ain't goin' to school to-day. She's afraid Mr. Starr will put Ida in if she don't; but there ain't no need of her worryin'; mebbe a way will be opened. I want you to lookout she don't go. There ain't no need of it."

"I'll do the best I can," said Amanda, with a doubtful glance at Lois.

Lois said nothing, but her pale little mouth contracted obstinately. She and Amanda followed her mother to the door. The departing woman said good-by, and went down the steps over the terraces. She never looked back. She went on out the gate, and turned into the long road. She had a mile walk to the railroad station.

Amanda and Lois went back into the sitting-room.

"When did she tell you she was going?" Lois asked suddenly.

"Last night."

"She didn't tell me till this morning."

Lois held her head high, but her eyes were surprised and pitiful, and the corners of her mouth drooped. She faced about to the window with a haughty motion, and watched her mother out of sight, a gaunt, dark old figure disappearing under low green elm branches.

CHAPTER III

It was many years since Mrs. Field had taken any but the most trivial journeys. Elliot was a hundred and twenty miles away. She must go to Boston; then cross the city to the other depot, where she would take the Elliot train. This elderly unsophisticated woman might very reasonably have been terrified at the idea of taking this journey alone, but she was not. She never thought of it.

The latter half of the road to the Green River station lay through an unsettled district. There were acres of low birch woods and lusty meadow-lands. This morning they were covered with a gold-green dazzle of leaves. To one looking across them, they almost seemed played over by little green flames; now and then a young birch tree stood away from the others, and shone by itself like a very torch of spring. Mrs. Field walked steadily through it. She had never paused to take much thought of the beauty of nature; to-day a tree all alive and twinkling with leaves might, for all her notice, have been naked and stiff with frost.

She did not seem to walk fast, but her long steps carried her over the ground well. It was long before train-time when she came in sight of the little station with its projecting piazza roofs. She entered the ladies' room and bought her ticket, then she sat down and waited. There were two other women there — middle-aged countrywomen in awkward wool gowns and flat straw bonnets, with a certain repressed excitement in their homely faces. They were setting their large, faithful, cloth-gaitered feet a little outside their daily ruts, and going to visit some relatives in a neighboring town; they were almost overcome by the unusualness of it.

Jane Field was a woman after their kind, and the look on their faces had its grand multiple in the look on hers. She had not only stepped out of her rut, but she was going out of sight of it forever.

She sat there stiff and silent, her two feet braced against the floor, ready to lift her at the signal of the train, her black leather bag grasped firmly in her right hand.

The two women eyed her furtively. One nudged the other. "Know who that is?" she whispered. But neither of them knew. They were from the adjoining town, which this railroad served as well as Green River.

Sometimes Mrs. Field looked at them, but with no speculation; the next moment she looked in the same way upon the belongings of the little country depot — the battered yellow settees, the time-tables, the long stove in its tract of littered sawdust, the man's face in the window of the ticket-office.

"Dreadful cross-lookin', ain't she?" one of the women whispered in the other's ear.

Jane heard the whisper, and looked at them. The women gave each other violent pokes, they reddened and tittered nervously, then they tried to look out of the window with an innocent and absent air. But they need not have been troubled. Jane, although she heard the whisper perfectly, did not connect it with herself at all. She never thought much about her own appearance; this morning she had as little vanity as though she were dead.

When the whistle of the train sounded, the women all pushed anxiously out on the platform.

"Is this the train that goes to Boston?" Mrs. Field asked one of the other two.

"I s'pose so," she replied, with a reciprocative flutter. "I'm goin' to ask so's to be sure. I'm goin' to Dale."

"I always ask," her friend remarked, with decision.

When the train stopped, Mrs. Field inquired of a brakeman. She was hardly satisfied with his affirmative answer. "Are you the conductor?" said she, sternly peering.

The young fellow gave a hurried wave of his hand toward the conductor, "There he is, ma'am."

Mrs. Field asked him also, then she hoisted herself into the car. When she had taken her seat, she put the same question to a woman in front of her.

It was a five-hours' ride to Boston. Mrs. Field sat all the while in her place with her bag in her lap, and never stirred. There was a look of rigid preparation about her, as if all her muscles were strained for an instant leap.

Two young girls in an opposite seat noticed her and tittered. They had considerable merriment over her, twisting their pretty silly faces, and rolling their blue eyes in her direction, and then averting them with soft repressed chuckles.

Occasionally Mrs. Field looked over at them, thought of her Lois, and noted their merriment gravely. She never dreamed that they were laughing at her. If she had, she would not have considered it twice.

It was four o'clock when Mrs. Field arrived in Boston. She had been in the city but once before, when she was a young girl. Still she set out with no hesitation to walk across the city to the depot where she must take the cars for Elliot. She could not afford a carriage, and she would not trust herself in a street car. She knew her own head and her old muscles; she could allow for their limitations, and preferred to rely upon them.

Every few steps she stopped and asked a question as to her route, listening sharply to the reply. Then she went straight enough, speeding between the informers like guide-posts. This old provincial threaded the city streets as unappreciatively as she had that morning the country one. Once in a while the magnificence of some shop window, a dark flash of jet, or a flutter of lace on a woman's dress caught her eye, but she did not see it. She had nothing in common with anything of that kind; she had to do with the primal facts of life. Coming as she was out of the country quiet, she was quite unmoved by the thundering rush of the city streets. She might have been deaf and blind for all the impression it had upon her. Her own nature had grown so intense that it apparently had emanations, and surrounded her with an atmosphere of her own impenetrable to the world.

It was nearly five o'clock when she reached her station, and the train was ready. It was half-past five when she arrived in Elliot. She got off the train and stalked, as if with a definite object, around the depot platform. She did not for one second hesitate or falter. She went up to a man who was loading some trunks on a wagon, and asked him to direct her to Lawyer Tuxbury's office. Her voice was so abrupt and harsh that the man started.

"Cross the track, an' go up the street till you come to it, on the right-hand side," he answered. Then he stared curiously after her as she went on.

Lawyer Tuxbury's small neat sign was fastened upon the door of the L of a large white house. There was a green yard, and some newly started flower-beds. In one there was a clump of yellow daffodils. Two yellow-haired little girls were playing out in the yard. They both stood still, staring with large, wary blue eyes at Mrs. Field as she came up the path. She never glanced toward them.

She stood like a black-draped statue before the office door, and knocked. Nobody answered.

She knocked again louder. Then a voice responded "Come in." Mrs. Field turned the knob carefully, and opened the door. It led directly into the room. There was a dull oil-cloth carpet, some beetling cases of heavy books, a few old arm-chairs, and one battered leather easy-chair. A great desk stood against the farther wall, and a man was seated at it, with his back toward the door. He had white hair, to which the sunlight coming through the west window gave a red-gold tinge.

Mrs. Field stood still, just inside the door. Apart from anything else, the room itself had a certain awe-inspiring quality for her. She had never before been in a lawyer's office. She was fully possessed with the rural and feminine ignorance and holy fear of all legal appurtenances. From all her traditions, this office door should have displayed a grinning man or woman trap, which she must warily shun.

She eyed the dusty oil-cloth — the files of black books — the chairs — the man at the desk, with his gilded white head. He wrote on steadily, and never stirred for a minute. Then he again sang out, sharply, "Come in."

He was deaf, and had, along with his insensibility to sounds, that occasional abnormal perception of them which the deaf seem sometimes to possess. He often heard sounds when none were recognizable to other people.

Now, evidently having perceived no result from his first response, he had heard this second knock, which did not exist except in his own supposition and the waiting woman's intent. She had, indeed, just at this point said to herself that she would slip out and knock again if he did not look around. She had not the courage to speak. It was almost as if the deaf lawyer, piecing out his defective ears with a subtler perception, had actually become aware of her intention, which had thundered upon him like the knock itself.

Mrs. Field made an inarticulate response, and took a grating step forward. The old man turned suddenly and saw her. She stood back again; there was a shrinking stiffness about her attitude, but she looked him full in the face.

"Why, good-day!" he exclaimed. "Good-day, madam. I didn't hear you come in."

Mrs. Field murmured a good-day in return.

"Take a seat, madam." The lawyer had risen, and was advancing toward her. He was a small, sharp-eyed man, whose youthful agility had crystallized into a nervous pomposity. Suddenly he stopped short; he had passed a broad slant of dusty sunlight which had lain between him and his visitor, and he could see her face plainly. His own elongated for a second, his under jaw lopped, and his brows contracted. Then he stepped forward. "Why, Mrs. Maxwell!" said he; "how do you do?"

"I'm pretty well, thank you," replied Mrs. Field. She tried to bow, but her back would not bend.

"I am delighted to see you," said the lawyer. "I recognize you perfectly now. I should have before, if the sun had not been in my eyes. I never forget a face."

He took her by the hand, and shook it up and down effusively. Then he pushed forward the leather easy-chair with gracious insinuation. Mrs. Field sat down, bolt-upright, on the extreme verge of it.

The lawyer drew a chair to her side, seated himself, leaned forward until his face fronted hers, and talked. His manner was florid, almost bombastic. He had a fashion of working his face a good deal when he talked. He conversed quite rapidly and fluently, but was wont to interlard his conversation with what seemed majestically reflective pauses, during which he leaned back in his chair and tapped the arm slowly. In fact his flow of ideas failed him for a moment, his mind being so constituted that they came in rapid and temporary bursts, geyser fashion. He inquired when Mrs. Field arrived, was kindly circumstantial as to her health, touched decorously but not too mournfully upon the late Thomas Maxwell's illness and decease. He alluded to the letter which he had written her, mentioning as a singular coincidence that at the moment of her entrance he was engaged in writing another to her, to inquire if the former had been received.

He spoke in terms of congratulation of the property to which she had fallen heir, and intimated that further discussion concerning it, as a matter of business, had better be postponed until morning. Daniel Tuxbury was very methodical in his care for himself, and was loath to attend to any business after six o'clock.

Mrs. Field sat like a bolt of iron while the lawyer talked to her. Unless a direct question demanded it, she never spoke herself. But he did not seem to notice it; he had enough garnered-in complacency to delight himself, as a bee with its own honey. He rarely realized it when another person did not talk.

After one of his pauses, he sprang up with alacrity. "Mrs. Maxwell, will you be so kind as to excuse me for a moment?" said he, and went out of the office with a fussy hitch, as if he wore invisible petticoats. Mrs. Field heard his voice in the yard.

When he returned there was an old lady following in his wake. Mrs. Field saw her before he did. She came with a whispering of silk, but his deaf ears did not perceive that. He did not notice her at all until he had entered the office, then he saw Mrs. Field looking past him at the door, and turned himself.

He went toward her with a little flourish of words, but the old lady ignored him entirely. She held up her chin with a kind of ancient pertness, and eyed Mrs. Field. She was a small, straight-backed woman, full of nervous vibrations. She stood apparently still, but her black silk whispered all the time, and loose ends of black ribbon trembled. The black silk had an air of old gentility about it, but it was very shiny; there were many bows, but the ribbons were limp, having been pressed and dyed. Her face, yellow and deeply wrinkled, but sharply vivacious, was overtopped by a bunch of purple flowers in a nest of rusty black lace and velvet.

So far Mrs. Field had maintained a certain strained composure, but now her long, stern face began flushing beneath this old lady's gaze.

"I conclude you know this lady," said the lawyer, with a blandly facetious air to the new-comer.

At that she stepped forward promptly, with a jerk as if to throw off her irresolution, and a certain consternation. "Yes, I s'pose I do," said she, in a voice like a shrill high chirp. "It's Mis' Maxwell, ain't it — Edward's wife? How do you do, Esther? I hadn't seen you for so long, I wasn't quite sure, but I see who you are now. How do you do?"

"I'm pretty well, thank you," said Mrs. Field, with a struggle, putting her twisted hand into the other woman's, extended quiveringly in a rusty black glove.

"When did you come to town, Esther?"

"Jest now."

"Let me see, where from? I can't seem to remember the name of the place where you've been livin'. I know it, too."

"Green River."

"Oh, yes, Green River. Well, I'm glad to see you, Esther. You ain't changed much, come to look at you; not so much as I have, I s'pose. I don't expect you'd know me, would you?"

"I — don't know as I would." Mrs. Field recoiled from a lie even in the midst of falsehood.

The old lady's face contracted a little, but she could spring above her emotions. "Well, I don't s'pose you would, either," responded she, with fine alacrity. "I've grown old and wrinkled and yellow, though I ain't gray," with a swift glance at Mrs. Field's smooth curves of white hair. "You turned gray pretty young, didn't you, Esther?"

"Yes, I did."

The old lady's front hair hung in dark-brown spirals, a little bunch of them against either cheek, outside her bonnet. She set them dancing with a little dip of her head when she spoke again. "I thought you did," said she. "Well, you're comin' over to my house, ain't you, Esther? You'll find a good many changes there. My daughter Flora and I are all that's left now, you know, I s'pose."

Mrs. Field moved her head uncertainly. This old woman, with her straight demands for truth or falsehood, was torture to her.

"I suppose you'll come right over with me pretty soon," the

old lady went on. "I don't want to hurry you in your business with Mr. Tuxbury, but I suppose my nephew will be home, and —"

"I'm jest as much obliged to you, but I guess I'd better not. I've made some other plans," said Mrs. Field.

"Oh, we are going to keep Mrs. Maxwell with us to-night," interposed the lawyer. He had stood by smilingly while the two women talked.

"I'm jest as much obliged, but I guess I'd better not," repeated Mrs. Field, looking at both of them.

The old lady straightened herself in her flimsy silk draperies. "Well, of course, if you've got other plans made, I ain't goin' to urge you, Esther," said she; "but any time you feel disposed to come, you'll be welcome. Good-evenin', Esther. Good-evenin', Mr. Tuxbury." She turned with a rustling bob, and was out the door.

The lawyer pressed forward hurriedly. "Why, Mrs. Maxwell, weren't you coming in? Isn't there something I can do for you?" said he.

"No, thank you," replied the old lady, shortly. "I've got to go home; it's my tea-time. I was goin' by, and I thought I'd jest look in a minute; that was all. It wa'n't anything. Good-evenin'." She was half down the walk before she finished speaking. She never looked around.

The lawyer turned to Mrs. Field. "Mrs. Henry Maxwell was not any too much please to see you sitting here," he whispered, with a confidential smile. "She wouldn't say anything; she's as proud as Lucifer; but she was considerably taken aback."

Mrs. Field nodded. She felt numb. She had not understood who this other woman was. She knew now — the mother of the young woman who was the rightful heir to Thomas Maxwell's property.

"The old lady has been pretty anxious," Mr. Tuxbury went on. "She's been in here a good many times — made excuses to come in and see if I had any news. She has been twice as much concerned as her daughter about it. Well, she has had a pretty hard time. That branch of the family lost a good deal of property."

Mrs. Field rose abruptly. "I guess I'd better be goin'," said she. "It must be your tea-time. I'll come in again to-morrow."

The lawyer put up his hand deprecatingly. "Mrs. Maxwell, you will, of course, stay and take tea with us, and remain with us to-night."

"I'm jest as much obliged to you for invitin' me, but I guess I'd better be goin'."

"My sister is expecting you. You remember my sister, Mrs. Lowe. I've just sent word to her. You had better come right over to the house with me now, and to-morrow morning we can attend to business. You must be fatigued with your journey."

"I'm real sorry if your sister's put herself out, but I guess I'd better not stay."

The lawyer turned his ear interrogatively. "I beg your pardon, but I didn't quite understand. You think you can't stay?"

"I'm — much obliged to your sister an' you for invitin' me, but — I guess — I'd better — not."

"Why — but — Mrs. Maxwell! Just be seated again for a moment, and let me speak to my sister; perhaps she —"

"I'm jest as much obliged to her, but I feel as if I'd better be goin'." Mrs. Field stood before him, mildly unyielding. She seemed to waver toward his will, but all the time she abided toughly in her own self like a willow bough. "But, Mrs. Maxwell, what *can* you do?" said the lawyer, his manner full of perplexity, and impatience thinly veiled by courtesy. "The hotel here is not very desirable, and —"

"Can't I go right up to — the house?"

"The Maxwell house?"

"Yes, sir; if there ain't anything to hinder."

Mr. Tuxbury stared at her. "Why, I don't know that there is really anything to hinder," he said, slowly. "Although it is rather — No, I don't know as there is any actual objection to your going. I suppose the house belongs to you. But it is shut up. I think you would find it much pleasanter here, Mrs. Maxwell." His eyebrows were raised, his mouth pursed up.

"I guess I'd better go, if I can jest as well as not; if I can get into the house." Mrs. Field spoke with deprecating persistency.

Mr. Tuxbury turned abruptly toward his desk, and began fumbling in a drawer. She stood hesitatingly watchful. "If you would jest tell me where I'd find the key," she ventured to remark. She had a vague idea that she would be told to look under a parlor blind for the key, that being the innocent country hiding-place when the house was left alone.

"I have the key, and I will go to the house with you myself directly."

"I hate to make you so much trouble. I guess I could find it myself, if —"

"I will be ready immediately, Mrs. Maxwell," said the lawyer, in a smoothly conclusive voice which abashed her.

She stood silently by the door until he was ready. He took her black bag peremptorily, and they went side by side down the street. He held his head well back, his lips were still tightly pursed, and he swung his cane with asperity. His important and irascible nature was oddly disturbed by this awkwardly obstinate old woman stalking at his side in her black clothes. Feminine opposition, even in slight matters, was wont to aggravate him, but in no such degree as this. He found it hard to recover his usual courtesy of manner, and indeed scarcely spoke a word during the walk. He could not himself understand his discomposure. But Mrs. Field did not seem to notice. She walked on, with her stern, impassive old face set straight ahead. Once they met a young girl who made her think of Lois, her floating draperies brushed against her black gown, for a second there was a pale, innocent little face looking up into her own.

It was not a very long walk to the Maxwell house.

"Here we are," said the lawyer, coldly, and unlatched a gate, and held it open with stiff courtesy for his companion to pass.

They proceeded in silence up the long curve of walk which led to the front door. The walk was brown and slippery with pine needles. Tall old pine trees stood in groups about the yard. There were also elm and horse-chestnut trees. The horse-chestnuts were in blossom, holding up their white bouquets, which showed dimly. It was now quite dusky.

Back of the trees the house loomed up. It was white and bulky, with fluted cornices and corner posts, and a pillared porch to the front door. Mrs. Field passed between the two outstanding pillars, which reared themselves whitely over her, like ghostly sentries, and stood waiting while Mr. Tuxbury fitted the key to the lock.

It took quite a little time; he could not see very well, he had forgotten his spectacles in his impatient departure. But at last he jerked open the door, and a strange conglomerate odor, the very breath of the life of the old Maxwell house, steamed out in their faces.

All bridal and funeral feasts, all daily food, all garments which had hung in the closets and rustled through the rooms, every piece of furniture, every carpet and hanging had a part in it.

The rank and bitter emanations of life, as well as spices and sweet herbs and delicate perfumes, went to make up the breath which smote one in the face upon the opening of the door. Still it was not a disagreeable, but rather a suggestive and poetical odor, which should affect one like a reminiscent dream. However, the village people sniffed at it, and said "How musty that old house is!"

That was what Daniel Tuxbury said now. "The house is musty," he remarked, with stately nose in the air.

Mrs. Field made no response. She stepped inside at once. "I'm much obliged to you," said she.

The lawyer looked at her, then past her into the dark depths of the house. "You can't see," said he. "you must let me go in with you and get a light." He spoke in a tone of short politeness. He was in his heart utterly out of patience with this strange, stiff old woman.

"I guess I can find one. I hate to make you so much trouble."

Mr. Tuxbury stepped forward with decision, and began fumbling in his pocket for a match. "Of course you cannot find one in the dark, Mrs. Maxwell," said he, with open exasperation.

She said nothing more, but stood meekly in the hall until a light flared out from a room on the left. The lawyer had found a lamp, he was himself somewhat familiar with the surroundings, but on the way to it he stumbled over a chair with an exclamation. It sounded like an oath to Mrs. Field, but she thought she must be mistaken. She had never in her life heard many oaths, and when she did had never been able to believe her ears.

"I hope you didn't hurt you," said she, deprecatingly, stepping forward.

"I am not hurt, thank you." But the twinge in the lawyer's ankle was confirming his resolution to say nothing more to her on the subject of his regret and unwillingness that she should choose to refuse his hospitality, and spend such a lonely and uncomfortable night. "I won't say another word to her about it," he declared to himself. So he simply made arrangements with her for a meeting at his office the next morning to attend to the business for which there had been no time to-night, and took his leave.

"I never saw such a woman," was his conclusion of the story, which he related to his sister upon his return home. His sister was a widow, and just then her married daughter and two children were visiting her.

"I wish you'd let me know she wa'n't comin'," said she. "I cut the fruit cake an' opened a jar of peach, an' I've put clean sheets on the front chamber bed. It's made considerable work for nothin'." She eyed, as she spoke, the two children, who were happily eating the peach preserve. She and her brother were both quite well-to-do, but she had a parsimonious turn.

"I'd like to know what she'll have for supper," she remarked further.

"I didn't ask her," said the lawyer, dryly, taking a sip of his sauce. He was rather glad of the peach himself.

"I shouldn't think she'd sleep a wink, all alone in that great old house. I know I shouldn't," observed the children's mother. She was a fair, fleshy, quite pretty young woman.

"That woman would sleep on a tomb-stone if she set out to," said the lawyer. His speech, when alone with his own household, was more forcible and not so well regulated. Indeed, he did not come of a polished family; he was the only educated one among them. His sister, Mrs. Low, regarded him with all the deference and respect which her own decided and self-sufficient character could admit of, and often sounded his praises in her unrestrained New England dialect.

"She seemed like a real set kind of a woman, then?" said she now.

"Set is no name for it," replied her brother.

"Well, if that's so, I guess old Mr. Maxwell wa'n't so far wrong when he didn't have her down here before," she remarked, with a judicial air. Her spectacles glittered, and her harsh, florid face bent severely over the sugar-bowl and the cups and saucers.

The lamp-light was mellow in the neat, homely dining-room, and there was a soft aroma of boiling tea all about. The pink and white children ate their peach sauce in happy silence, with their pretty eyes upon the prospective cake.

"I suppose there must be some bed made up in all that big house," remarked their mother; "but it must be awful lonesome."

Of the awful lonesomeness of it truly, this smiling, comfortable young soul had no conception. At that moment, while they were drinking their tea and talking her over, Jane Field sat bolt-upright in one of the old flag-bottomed chairs in the Maxwell sitting-room. She had dropped into it when the lawyer closed the door after him, and she never stirred afterward. She sat there all night.

The oil was low in the lamp which the lawyer had lighted, and left standing on the table between the windows. She could see distinctly for a while the stately pieces of old furniture standing in their places against the walls. Just opposite where she sat was one of lustreless old mahogany, extending the width of the wall between two doors, rearing itself upon slender legs, set with multitudinous drawers, and surmounted by a clock. A piece of furniture for which she knew no name, an evidence of long-established wealth and old-fashioned luxury, of which she and her plain folk, with their secretaries and desks and bureaus, had known nothing. The clock had stopped at three o'clock. Mrs. Field thought to herself that it might have been the hour on which old Mr. Maxwell died, reflecting that souls were more apt to pass away in the wane of the night. She would have like to wind the clock, and set the hands moving past that ghostly hour, but she did not dare to stir. She gazed at the large, dull figures sprawling over the old carpet, at the glimmering satiny scrolls on the wall-paper. On the mantel-shelf stood a branching gilt candlestick, filled with colored candles, and strung around with prisms, which glittered feebly in the low lamp-light. There was a bulging, sheet-iron wood stove — the Maxwells had always eschewed coal; beside it lay a little pile of sticks, brought in after the chill of death had come over the house. There were a few old engravings — a head of Washington, the Landing of the Pilgrims, the Webster death-bed scene, and one full-length portrait of the old statesman, standing majestically, scroll in hand, in a black frame.

As the oil burned low, the indistinct figures upon the carpet and wall-paper grew more indistinct, the brilliant colors of the prisms turned white, and the fine black and white lights in the death-bed picture ran together.

Finally the lamp went out. Mrs. Field had spied matches over on the shelf, but she did not dare to rise to cross the room to get them and find another lamp. She did not dare to stir.

After her light went out, there was still a pale glimmer upon the opposite wall, and the white face of the silent clock showed out above the cumbersome shadow of the great mahogany piece. The glimmer came from a neighbor's lamp shining through a gap in the trees. Soon that also went out, and the old woman sat there in total darkness.

She folded her hands primly, and held up her bonneted head in the darkness, like some decorous and formal caller who might expect at any moment to hear the soft, heavy step of the host upon the creaking stair and his voice in the room. She sat there so all night.

Gradually this steady-headed, unimaginative old woman became possessed by a legion of morbid fancies, which played like wild fire over the terrible main fact of the case — the fact that underlay everything — that she had sinned, that she had gone over from good to evil, and given up her soul for a handful of gold. Many a time in the night, voices which her straining fancy threw out, after the manner of ventriloquism, from her own brain, seemed actually to vibrate through the house, footsteps pattered, and garments rustled. Often the phantom noises would swell to a very pandemonium surging upon her ears; but she sat there rigid and resolute in the midst of it, her pale old face sharpening out into the darkness. She sat there, and never stirred until morning broke.

When it was fairly light, she got up, took off her bonnet and shawl, and found her way into the kitchen. She washed her face and hands at the sink, and went deliberately to work getting herself some breakfast. She had a little of her yesterday's lunch left; she kindled a fire, and made a cup of tea. She found some in a caddy in the pantry. She set out her meal on the table and drew a chair before it. She had wound up the kitchen clock, and she listened to its tick while she ate. She took time, and finished her slight repast to the last crumb. Then she washed the dishes, and swept and tidied the kitchen.

When that was done it was still too early for her to go to the lawyer's office. She sat down at an open kitchen window and folded her hands. Outside was a broad, green yard, inclosed on two sides by the Maxwell house and barn. A drive-way led to the barn, and on the farther side a row of apple-trees stood. There was a fresh wind blowing, and the apple blossoms were floating about. The drive was quite white with them in places, and they were half impaled upon the sharp green blades of grass.

Over through the trees Mrs. Field could see the white top of a market wagon in a neighboring yard, and the pink dress of a woman who stood beside it trading. She watched them with a dull wonder. What had she now to do with market wagons and daily meals and housewifely matters? That fair-haired woman in the pink dress seemed to her like a woman of another planet.

This narrow-lived old country woman could not consciously moralize. She was no philosopher, but she felt, without putting it into thoughts, as if she had descended far below the surface of all things, and found out that good and evil were the root and the life of them, and the outside leaves and froth and flowers were fathoms away, and no longer to be considered.

At ten o'clock she put on her bonnet and shawl, and set out for the lawyer's office. She locked the front door, put the key under a blind, and proceeded down the front walk into the street.

The spring was earlier here than in Green River. She started at a dancing net-work of leaf shadows on the sidewalk. They were the first she had seen that season. There was a dewy arch of trees overhead, and they were quite fully leaved out. Mr. Tuxbury was in his office when she got there. He rose promptly and greeted her, and pushed forward the leather easy-chair with his old courtly flourish.

"I suppose that old stick of a woman will be in pretty soon," he had remarked to his sister at breakfast-time.

"Well, you'll keep on the right side of her, if you know which side your bread is buttered," she retorted. "You don't want her goin' to Sam Totten's."

Totten was the other lawyer of Elliot.

"I think I am quite aware of all the exigencies of the case," Daniel Tuxbury had replied, lapsing into stateliness, as he always did when his sister waxed too forcible in her advice.

But when Mrs. Field entered his office, every trace of his last night's impatience had vanished. He inquired genially if she had passed a comfortable night, and on being assured that she had, pressed her to drink a cup of coffee which he had requested his sister to keep warm. This declined, with her countrified courtesy, so shy that it seemed grim, he proceeded, with no chill upon his graciousness, to business.

Through the next two hours Mrs. Field sat at the lawyer's desk, and listened to a minute and wearisome description of her new possessions. She listened with very little understanding. She did not feel any interest in it. She never opened her mouth except now and then for a stiff assent to a question from the lawyer.

A little after twelve o'clock he leaned back in his chair with a conclusive sigh, and fixed his eyes reflectively upon the ceiling. "Well, Mrs. Maxwell," said he, "I think that you understand pretty well now the extent and the limitations of your property."

"Yes, sir," said she.

"It is all straight enough. Maxwell was a good business man; he kept his affairs in excellent order. Yes, he was a very good business man."

Suddenly the lawyer straightened himself, and fixed his eyes with genial interest upon his visitor; business over, he had a mind for a little personal interview to show his good-will. "Let me see, Mrs. Maxwell, you had a sister, did you not?" said he.

"Yes, sir."

"Is she living?"

"No, sir." Mrs. Field said it with a gasping readiness to speak one truth.

"Let me see, what was her name?" asked the lawyer. "No; wait a moment; I'll tell you. I've heard it." He held up a hand as if warding off an answer from her, his face became furrowed with reflective wrinkles. "Field!" cried he, suddenly, with a jerk, and beamed at her. "I thought I could remember it," said he. "Yes, your sister's name was Field. When did she die, Mrs. Maxwell?"

"Two years ago."

There was a strange little smothered exclamation from some one near the office door. Mrs. Field turned suddenly, and saw her daughter Lois standing there.

CHAPTER IV

There Lois stood. Her small worn shoes hesitated on the threshold. She was gotten up in her poor little best — her dress of cheap brown wool stuff, with its skimpy velvet panel, her hat trimmed with a fold of silk and a little feather. She had curled her hair over her forehead, and tied on a bit of a lace veil. Distinct among all this forlorn and innocent furbishing was her face, with its pitiful, youthful prettiness, turning toward her mother and the lawyer with a very clutch of vision.

Mrs. Field got up. "Oh, it's you, Lois," she said, calmly. "You thought you'd come too, didn't you?"

Lois gasped out something.

Her mother turned to the lawyer. "I'll make you acquainted with Miss Lois Field," said she. "Lois, I'll make you acquainted with Mr. Tuxbury."

The lawyer was looking surprised, but he rose briskly to the level of the situation, and greeted the young girl with ready grace. "Your sister's daughter, I conclude," he said, smilingly, to Mrs. Field.

Mrs. Field set her mouth hard. She looked defiantly at him and said not one word. There was a fierce resolve in her heart that, come what would, she would not tell this last lie, and deny her daughter before her very face.

But the lawyer did not know she was silent. Not having heard any response, with the vanity of a deaf man, he assumed that she had given one, and so concealed his uncertainty.

"Yes, so I thought," said he, and went on flourishingly in his track of gracious reception.

Lois kept her eyes fixed on his like some little timid animal which suspects an enemy, and watches his eyes for the first impetus of a spring. Once or twice she said, "Yes, sir," faintly.

"Your niece does not look very strong," Mr. Tuxbury said to Mrs. Field.

"She ain't been feelin' very well this spring. I've been considerable worried about her," she answered, with harsh decision.

"Ah, I am very sorry to hear that. Well, she will soon recuperate if she stays here. Elliot is considered a very healthy place. We shall soon have her so hearty and rosy that her old friends won't be able to recognize her." He bowed with a smiling flourish to Lois.

Her lips trembled with a half-smile in response, but she looked more frightened than ever.

"Now, Mrs. Maxwell," said the lawyer, "you and your niece must positively remain and dine with us to-day, can't you?"

"I'm afraid it will put your sister out."

"Oh, no, indeed." The lawyer, however, had a slightly non-plussed expression. "She will be delighted. I will run over to the house, then, and tell her that you will stay, shall I not?"

"I hate to make her extra work," said Mrs. Field. That was her rural form of acceptance.

"You will not, I assure you. Don't distress yourself about that, Mrs. Maxwell."

Nevertheless, he was quite ill at ease as he traversed the yard. In his life with his sister there were exigencies during which he was obliged to descend from his platform of superiority. He foresaw the approach of one now.

Dinner was already served when he entered the dining-room, and his sister was setting the chairs around the table. They kept no servant.

"They are going to stay to dinner, I expect," he remarked, in a appealingly confidential tone.

His sister faced him with a jerk. She was very red from bending over the kitchen fire. "Who's goin' to stay? What do you mean, Daniel?"

"Why, Mrs. Maxwell and her niece."

"Her niece? I didn't know she had any niece. How did she get here?"

"She came this noon; followed along after her aunt, I suppose. I don't think she knew she was coming. She acted kind of surprised, I thought."

"You don't mean they're comin' in here to dinner?"

"I couldn't very well help asking them, you know." His tone was soft and conciliatory, and he kept a nervous eye upon his sister's face.

"Couldn't help askin' 'em! I ruther guess I could 'a' helped askin' 'em!"

"Jane, I hadn't any idea they'd stay."

"Well, you've gone an' done it, that's all I've got to say. Here they didn't come last night, when I got all ready for 'em, an' now they're comin', an' everything we've got is a picked-up dinner; there ain't enough of anything to go round. Flora!"

Her daughter Flora came in from the kitchen, with the children, in blue gingham aprons, at her heels.

"What is it, mother?" said she.

"Nothin', only your uncle Daniel has asked that Maxwell

woman an' her niece to dinner, an' they're goin' to stay."

"My goodness! there isn't a thing for dinner!" said Flora, with a half-giggle. She was so young and healthy and happy that she could still see the joke in an annoyance.

Her uncle looked at her beseechingly. "Can't you manage somehow?" said he. "I'll go down to the store and buy something."

"Down to the store!" repeated his sister, contemptuously. "It's one o'clock now."

He looked at the kitchen clock, visible through the open door, and saw that it indicated half-past twelve, but he said nothing.

Flora was frowning reflectively, while her cheeks dimpled. "I tell you what I'll do, mother," said she. "I'll go over to Mrs. Bennett's and borrow a pie. I think we can get along if we have a pie."

"I ain't goin' round the neighborhood borrowin'; that ain't the way I'm accustomed to doin'."

"Land, mother! I'd just as soon ask Mrs. Bennett as not. She borrowed that bread in here the other night."

"There ain't enough steak to go round; there's jest that little piece we had left from yesterday, an' there ain't enough stew," said her mother, with persistent wrath.

"Well, if folks come in unexpectedly, they'll have to take what we've got and make the best of it." Flora tied a hat on over her light hair as she spoke. "I don't see any other way for them," she added, laughingly, going out of the door.

"It's all very well for folks to be easy," said her mother, with a sniff, "but when she's had as much as I've had, I guess she won't take it any easier than I do. I s'pose now I've got to take all these things off, an' put on a clean table-cloth."

"That one doesn't look very bad," ventured her brother, timidly.

"No, I shouldn't think it did! Look at that great coffee stain you got on it this mornin'! Havin' a couple of perfect strangers come in to dinner makes more work than a man knows anything about. Children, you take off the knives, an' pile 'em up on the other table. Be real careful."

"I wonder if the parlor's so I can ask them in there?" Mr. Tuxbury remarked, edging toward the door.

"I s'pose so. I ain't been in there this mornin'; I s'pose it's all right unless the children have been in an' cluttered it up."

"No, we ain't, gramma, we ain't," proclaimed the children in a shrill shout. They danced around the table, removing the knives and forks; their innocent, pinky faces were full of cherubic glee.

This occasion was, metaphorically speaking, a whole flock of jubilant infantile larks for them. They loved company with all their souls, and they also felt always a pleasant titillation of their youthful spirits when they saw their grandmother in perturbation. Unless, indeed, they themselves were the cause of it, when it acquired a personal force which rendered it not so entertaining.

Soon, however, a remark of their grandmother's caused their buoyant spirits to realize that there was a force of gravitation for all here below.

"I don't know but you children will have to wait," said she.

There was an instantaneous wail of dismay, the pinky faces elongated, the blue eyes scowled sulkily. "Oh, gramma, we don't want to wait! Can't we sit down with the others? Say, gramma, can't we? Can't we sit down with the others?"

"Of course you can sit down with the others. Don't make such a racket, children." That was their mother coming in, good-natured and triumphant, with the pie.

"I don't know whether they can or not," said their grandmother. "I ain't put in an extra leaf; this table-cloth wa'n't long enough, an' I wa'n't goin' to have the big table-cloth to do up for all the Maxwells in creation."

"Oh, there's room enough," Flora said, easily. "I can squeeze them in beside me. Put the napkins round, children, and stop teasing. Didn't I get a beautiful pie?"

"What kind is it?"

"Squash."

"An' our squashes are all gone, an' I've got to buy one to pay her back. I should have thought you'd known better, Flora."

"It was all the kind she had. I couldn't help it. Squashes don't cost much, mother."

"They cost something, an' I've got all them dried apples to use up for pies."

"Have they come in?" asked Flora, with happy unconcern about the cost of squashes and the utilization of dried apples.

"Yes, I s'pose so. I thought I heard Daniel taking 'em in the front door. I s'pose they're in the parlor."

"You ought to go in a minute, hadn't you?"

"I s'pose so," replied Mrs. Lowe, with a sigh of fierce resignation.

"I'll finish setting the things on the table, and you go in. Take off your apron."

"This dress don't look fit."

"Yes, it does, too; it's clean. Run along."

Mrs. Lowe smoothed her sparse hair severely at the kitchen looking-glass; then she advanced upon the parlor with the air of a pacific grenadier. The children were following slyly in her wake, but their mother caught sight of them and pulled them back.

Mr. Tuxbury had been sitting in the parlor with his guests, trying his best to entertain them. He had gotten out the photograph album for Lois, and a book of views in the Holy Land for her mother. If he had felt in considerable haste to escape from his sister's indignation and return to his visitors, they had been equally anxious for him to come.

When Mrs. Field and her daughter were left alone in the office, their first sensation was that of actual terror of each other.

Mrs. Field concealed hers well enough. She sat up without a tremor in her unbending back, and looked out of the office door, which the lawyer had left open. Just opposite the door, out on the sidewalk, two men stood talking. She kept her eyes fastened upon them.

"What time did you start?" said she presently, in a harsh voice, which seemed to rudely shock the stillness. She did not turn her eyes.

"I — came — on the first — train," answered Lois, pantingly. Once in a while she stole furtive, wildly questioning glances at her mother, but her mother never met them. She continued to look at the talking men on the sidewalk.

"Mother," began Lois finally, in a desperate voice. But just then Mr. Tuxbury had reappeared, and conducted them to his parlor.

The parlor had lace curtains and a Brussles carpet, and looked ornate to Mrs. Field and Lois. The chairs were covered with green plush. The two women sat timidly on the yielding cushions, and gazed during the pauses at the large flower pattern on the carpet. All this fine furniture was, in fact, Mrs. Lowe's; when she had given up her own home, and come to live with her brother, she had brought it with her.

Both of the guests arose awkwardly, Mrs. Field first and Lois after her, when Mrs. Lowe entered, and the lawyer introduced them.

"I'm happy to make your acquaintance," said Mrs. Field.

"I believe I've seen you two or three times when you was here years ago," said Mrs. Lowe, standing before her straight and tall in her faded calico gown, which fitted her uncompromisingly like a cuirass. Mrs. Lowe's gowns, no matter how thin and faded, always fitted her in that way. Stretched over her long flat-chested figure, they seemed to acquire the consistency of armor. "You ain't changed any as I can see," she went on, as she got scarcely any response to her first remark. "I should have known you anywhere. It's a pleasant day, ain't it?"

"Real pleasant," replied Mrs. Field. Mrs. Lowe sat down in one of the plush chairs. To seat herself for a few minutes before announcing dinner was, she supposed, a matter of etiquette. She held up her long rasped chin with a curt air, and, in spite of herself, her voice also was curt. She was too thorough a New England woman to play with any success softening lights over the steel of her character. She disdained to, and she was also unable to. She was not pleased to receive these unexpected guests, and she showed it.

As soon as she thought it decently practicable, she gave a significant look at her brother and arose. "I guess we'll walk out to dinner now," said she, with solemn embarrassment. Mrs. Lowe had nothing of her brother's ease of manner; indeed, she entertained a covert scorn for it. "Daniel *can be dreadful smooth an' fine when he sets out," she sometimes remarked to her daughter. The lawyer's suave manner seemed to her downrightness to border upon affectation. She, however, had a certain respect for it as the probable outcome of his superior education.*

She marched ahead stiffly now, and left her brother to his flourishing seconding of her announcement. Flora and the children received them beamingly when they entered the dining-room. Flora was quite sure that she remembered Mrs. Maxwell, she was glad to see her, and she was glad to see Lois, and they would please sit right "here," and "here." She had taken off the children's pinafores and washed their faces, and they stood aloof in little starched and embroidered frocks, with their cheeks pinker than ever.

Flora seated one on each side of her, as she had said. "Now, you must be good and not tease," she whispered admonishingly, and their blue eyes stared back at her with innocent gravity, and they folded their small hands demurely.

Nevertheless, it was through them that the whole dignity of the meal was lost. If they had not been present, it would have passed off with a strong undercurrent of uneasiness and discomfort, yet with composure. Mr. Tuxbury would have helped the guests to beefsteak, and the rest of the family would have preferred the warmed-up veal stew. Or had the guests looked approvingly at the stew, the scanty portion of beefsteak would have satisfied the furthest desires of the family. But the perfect understanding among the adults did not extend to the two little girls. They leaned forward, with their red lips parted, and watched their uncle anxiously as he carved the beefsteak. There was evidently not much of it, and their anxiety grew. When it was separated into three portions, two of which were dispensed to the guests, and the other, having been declined by their grandmother and mother, was appropriated by their uncle, anxiety lapsed into certainty.

"I want some beefsteak!" wailed each, in wofully injured tones.

Mr. Tuxbury set his mouth hard, and pushed his plate with a jerk toward his niece. Her face was very red, but she took it — she was aware there was no other course open — divided the meat impartially, and gave each child a piece with a surreptitious thump.

Mr. Tuxbury, with a moodily knitted forehead and a smiling mouth, asked the guests miserably if they would have some veal stew. It was perfectly evident that if they accepted, there would be nothing whatever left for the family to eat. They declined in terrified haste; indeed, both Lois and her mother had been impelled to pass their portions of beefsteak over to the children, but they had not dared.

The children wished for veal stew also, and when they had eaten their meagre spoonfuls, clamored persistently for more.

"There isn't any more," whispered their mother, with two little vigorous side-shakes. "If you don't keep still, I shall take you away from the table. Ain't you ashamed?"

Then the little girls pouted and sniffed, but warily, lest the threat be carried into effect.

The rest of the family tried to ignore the embarrassing situation and converse easily with the guests, but it was a difficult undertaking.

Lois bent miserably over her plate, and every question appeared to shock her painfully. She seemed an obstinately bashful young girl, to whom it was useless to talk. Mrs. Field replied at length to all interrogations with a certain quiet hardness, which had come into her manner since her daughter's arrival, but she never started upon a subject of her own accord.

It was a relief to every one when the meagre dinner lapsed into the borrowed pie. Mrs. Low cut it carefully into the regulation six pieces, while the children as carefully counted the people and watched the distribution. The result was not satisfactory. The older little girl, whose sense of injury was well developed, set up a shrill demand.

"I want a piece of Mis' Bennett's pie," said she. "Mother, I want a piece of Mis' Bennett's pie!"

The younger, viewing the one piece of pie remaining in the plate and her clamorous sister, raised her own jealous little pipe. "I want a piece of Mis' Bennett's pie," she proclaimed, pulling her mother's sleeve. "Mother, can't I have a piece of Mis' Bennett's pie?"

Flora's face was very red, and her mouth was twitching. She hastily pushed her own pie to the elder child, and gave the last piece on the plate to the younger. Their grandmother frowned on them like a rock, but they ate their pie unconcernedly.

"I think Mis' Bennett's pie is a good deal better than grandma's," said the younger little girl, smacking her lips contemplatively; and Flora gave a half-chuckle, while her mother's severity of mien so deepened that she seemed to cast an actual shadow.

"Now, Flora, I tell you what 'tis," said she, when the meal was at last over and the guests were gone — they took their leave very soon afterward — "if you don't punish them children, I shall."

There was a wail of terror from the little girls. "Oh, mother, you do it, you do it!" cried they.

Flora giggled audibly.

"You'll just spoil them children," said her mother, severely; "you ought to be ashamed of yourself, Flora."

Flora tried to draw her face into gravity. "Go right upstairs, children," said she. "It's so funny, I can't help it," she whispered, with another furtive giggle.

"I don't see anything very funny in children's actin' the way they have all dinner-time."

The children thumped merrily over the stairs. It was clear that they stood in no great fear of their mother's chastisement. They knew by experience that her hand was very soft, and the force of its fall tempered by mirth and tender considerateness; their grandmother's fleshless and muscular old palm was another matter.

Soon after Flora followed them there was a series of arduous cries, apparently maintained more from a childish sense of the fitness of things than from any actual stress of pain. They soon ceased.

"She ain't half whipped 'em," Mrs. Lowe, who was listening downstairs, said to herself.

The lawyer was in his office; he had intrenched himself there as soon as possible, covering his retreat with the departure of his guests.

Mrs. Field and Lois, removed from it all the distance of tragedy from comedy, were walking up the street to the Maxwell house. Mrs. Field stalked ahead with her resolute stiffness; Lois followed after her, keeping always several paces behind. No matter how often Mrs. Field, sternly conscious of it, slackened her own pace, Lois never gained upon her.

When they reached the gate at the entrance of the Maxwell grounds, and Mrs. Field stopped, Lois spoke up.

"What place is this?" said she, in a defiantly timorous voice.

"The Maxwell house," replied her mother, shortly, turning up the walk.

"Are you going in here?"

"Of course I am."

"Well, I ain't going in one step."

Mrs. Field turned and faced her. "Lois," said she, "if you want to go away an' desert the mother that's showin' herself willin' to die for you, you can."

Lois said not another word. She turned in at the gate, with her eyes fixed upon her mother's face.

"I'll tell you about it when we get up to the house," said her mother, with appealing conciliation.

Lois slunk mutely behind her again. Her eyes were full of the impulse of flight when she watched her mother unlock the house door, but she followed her in.

Her mother led the way into the sitting-room. "Sit down," said she.

And Lois sat down in the nearest chair. She never took her eyes off her mother.

Mrs. Field took off her bonnet and shawl. She folded the shawl carefully in the creases, and laid it on the table. She pulled up a curtain. Then she turned, and confronted steadily her daughter's eyes. The whole house to her was full of the clamor of their questioning. "Now, Lois," said Mrs. Field, "I'm goin' to tell you about this. I s'pose you think it's funny."

"I don't know what to think of it," said Lois, in a dry voice.

"I don't s'pose you do. Well, I'm goin' to tell you. You know, I s'pose, that Mr. Tuxbury took me for your aunt Esther. You heard him call me Mis' Maxwell?"

Lois nodded; her dilated eyes never wavered from her mother's face.

"I s'pose you heard what he was sayin' to me when you come

in. Lois, I didn't tell him I was your aunt Esther. The minute I come in, he took me for her, an' Mis' Henry Maxwell come into his office, an' she did, and so did Mr. Tuxbury's sister. I wa'n't goin' to tell them I wa'n't her."

The impulse of flight in Lois' watchful eyes became so strong that it seemed almost to communicate to her muscles. With her face still turned toward her mother, she appeared to be fleeing from her.

Mrs. Field stood her ground stanchly. "No, I wa'n't," she went on. "An' I'll tell you why. I'm goin' to have that fifteen hundred dollars of your poor father's earnin's that I lent your uncle out of this property, an' this is all the way to do it, an' I'm goin' to do it."

"I thought," gasped Lois — "I thought maybe it belonged to us anyway if Aunt Esther was dead."

"It didn't. The money was all left to old Mr. Maxwell's niece in case Esther died first."

"Couldn't you have asked the lawyer about the fifteen hundred dollars? Wouldn't he have given you some? O mother!"

"I was goin' to if he hadn't took me for her, but it wouldn't have done any good. They wouldn't have been obliged to pay it, an' folks ain't fond of payin' over money when they ain't obliged to. I'd been a fool to have asked him after he took me for her."

"Then — you'd got this — all planned?"

Her mother took her up sharply.

"No, I hadn't got it all planned," said she. "I don't deny it come into my head. I knew how much folks said I looked like Esther, but I didn't go so far as to plan it; there needn't anybody say I did."

"You ain't going to take the money?"

"I'm goin' to take that fifteen hundred dollars out of it."

"Mother, you ain't going to stay here, and make folks think you're Aunt Esther?"

"Yes, I am."

Then all Lois' horror and terror manifested themselves in one cry — "O mother!"

Mrs. Field never flinched. "If you want to act so an' feel so about it, you can," said she. "Your mother is some older than you, an' she knows what is right jest about as well as you can tell her. I've thought it all over. That fifteen hundred dollars was money your poor father worked hard to earn. I lent it to your uncle Edward, an' he lost it. I never see a dollar of it afterward. He never paid me a cent of interest money. It ain't anything more'n fair that I should be paid for it out of his father's property. If poor Esther had lived, the money'd gone to her, an' she'd paid me fast enough. Now the way's opened for me to get it, I ain't goin' to let it go. Talk about it's bein' right, if it ain't right to stoop down an' pick up anybody's just dues, I don't know what right is, for my part."

"Mother!"

"What say?"

"You ain't going to live here in this house, and not go back to Green River?"

"I don't see any need of goin' back to Green River. This is a 'nough sight prettier place than Green River. Now you're down here, I don't see any sense in layin' out money to go back at all. Mandy'll send our things down."

"You don't mean to stay right along here in this house, and not go back to Green River at all?"

"I don't see why it ain't jest as well. You'd better take off your things an' lay down a little while on that sofa there, an' get rested."

Lois seldom cried, but she burst out now in a piteous wail. "O mother," sobbed she, "what does it mean? I can't — What does it mean? Oh, I'm so frightened! Mother, you frighten me so! What does it mean?"

Her mother went up to her, and stood close at her side. "Lois," said she, with trembling solemnity, "can't you trust mother?"

"O mother, I don't know! I don't know! You frighten me dreadfully." Lois shrank away from her mother as she wept.

Mrs. Field stood over her, but she did not offer to touch her. Indeed, this New England mother and daughter rarely or never caressed each other. "Lois, dear child, mother don't want you to feel so. Oh, you dear child, you dear child, you don't know what mother's goin' through. But it ain't anything to you. Lois, you remember that; it ain't anything you've done. It's all my doin's. I'm jest goin' to get that money back. An' it's right I should. Don't you worry nothin' about it. Now take your hat off, an' let mother tuck you up on the sofa."

Lois, sobbing still, began pulling off her hat mechanically. Her mother got a pillow, and she lay down on the sofa, turning her face to the wall with another outburst of tears. Her mother spread her black shawl carefully over her.

"Now you lay here still, an' get rested," said she. "I'm goin' out in the kitchen, an' see if I can't start up a fire an' get something for supper."

Mrs. Field went out of the room. Soon her tall black figure sped stealthily past the windows out of the yard. She found a grocery store, and purchased some small necessaries. There were groceries already in the pantry at the Maxwell house. She had spied them, but would not touch a single article. She bought some tea, and when she returned, replaced the drawing she had taken that morning from the Maxwell caddy.

The old woman's will, always vigorous, never giving place to another except through its own choice, now whipped by this great stress into a fierce impetus, carried her daughter's, strong as it was for a young girl, before it. Lois lay quietly on the sofa. When her mother called her, she went out in the kitchen and ate her supper.

They retired early. Lois lay on the sofa until her mother came in and stood over her with a lighted lamp.

"I guess you'd better get up and go to bed now, Lois," said she. "I'm goin' myself, if it is early. I'm pretty tired."

And Lois stirred herself wearily and got up.

There were two adjoining bedrooms opening out of the sitting-room. Mrs. Field had prepared the beds that afternoon. "I thought we'd better sleep in here," said she, leading the way to them.

Lois had the inner room. After the lamp was blown out and everything was dark, her mother heard a soft stir and the pat of a naked foot in there, then she heard the door swing to with a cautious creak and the bolt slide. She knew with a great pang, that Lois had locked her door against her mother.

CHAPTER V

Elliot was only a little way from the coast, and sometimes seemed to be pervaded by the very spirit of the sea. The air would be full of salt vigor, the horizon sky take on the level, out-reaching blue of a water distance, and the clouds stand one way like white sails.

The next morning Lois sat on the front door-step of the Maxwell house, between the pillars of the porch. She bent over, leaning her elbows on her knees, making a cup of her hands, in which she rested her little face. She could smell the sea, and also the pines in the yard. There were many old pine trees, and their soft musical roar sounded high overhead. The spring air in Green River had been full of sweet moisture and earthiness from these steaming meadow-lands. Always in Green River, above the almond scent of the flowering trees and the live breath of the new grass, came that earthy, moist odor, like a reminder of the grave. Here in Elliot one smelled the spring above the earth.

The gate clicked, and a woman came up the curving path with a kind of clumsy dignity. She was tall and narrow-shouldered, but heavy-hipped; her black skirt flounced as she walked. She stopped in front of Lois, and looked at her hesitatingly. Lois arose.

"Good-mornin'," said the woman. Her voice was gentle; she cleared her throat a little after she spoke.

"Good-morning," returned Lois, faintly.

"Is Mis' Maxwell to home?"

Lois stared at her.

"Is Mis' Maxwell to home? I heard she'd come here to live," repeated the woman, in a deprecating way. She smoothed down the folds of her over-skirt. Lois started; the color spread over her face and neck. "No, she isn't at home," she said sharply.

"Do you know when she will be?"

"No, I don't."

The woman's face also was flushed. She turned about with a little flirt, when suddenly a door slammed somewhere in the house. The woman faced about, with a look of indignant surprise.

Lois said nothing. She opened the front door and went into the house, straight through to the kitchen, where her mother was preparing breakfast. "There's a woman out there," she said.

"Who is it?"

"I don't know. She wants to see — Mrs. Maxwell."

Lois looked full at her mother; her eyes were like an angel's before evil. Mrs. Field looked back at her. Then she turned toward the door.

Lois caught hold of her mother's dress. Mrs. Field twitched it away fiercely, and passed on into the sitting-room. The woman stood there waiting. She had followed Lois in.

"How do you do, Mis' Maxwell?" she said.

"I'm pretty well, thank you," replied Mrs. Field, looking at her with stiff inquiry.

The woman had a pale, pretty face, and stood with a sturdy set-back on her heels. "I guess you don't know me, Mis' Maxwell," said she, smiling deprecatingly.

Mrs. Field tried to smile, but her lips were too stiff. "I guess I — don't," she faltered.

The smile faded from the woman's face. She cast an anxious glance at her own face in the glass over the mantel-shelf; she had placed herself so she could see it. "I ain't got quite so much color as I used to have," she said, "but I ain't thought I'd changed much other ways. Some days I have more color. I know I ain't this mornin'. I ain't had very good health. Maybe that's the reason you don't know me."

Mrs. Field muttered a feeble assent.

"I'd know you anywhere, but you didn't have any color to lose to make a difference. You've always looked jest the way you do now since I've known you. I lived in this house a whole year with you once. I come here to live after Mr. Maxwell's wife died. My name is Jay."

Mrs. Field stood staring. The woman, who had been looking in the glass while she talked, gave her front hair a little shake, and turned toward her inquiringly.

"Won't you sit down in this rockin'-chair, Mis' Jay?" said Mrs. Field.

"No, thank you, I guess I won't set down, I'm in a little of a hurry. I jest wanted to see you a minute."

Mrs. Field waited.

"You know Mr. Maxwell's dyin' so sudden made a good deal of a change for me," Mrs. Jay continued. She took out her handkerchief and wiped her eyes softly; then she glanced in the glass. "I'd had my home here a good many years, an' it seemed hard to lose it all in a minute so. There he came home that Sunday noon an' eat a hearty dinner, an' before sunset he had that shock, and never spoke afterward. I've thought maybe there were things he would have said if he could have spoke."

Mrs. Jay sighed heavily; her eyes reddened; she straightened her bonnet absently; her silvered fair hair was frizzed under it.

Mrs. Field stood opposite, her eyes downcast, her face rigid.

"I wanted to speak to you, Mis' Maxwell," the other woman went on. "I ain't obliged to go out anywheres to live; I've got property; but it's kind of lonesome at my sister's, where I'm livin'. It's a little out of the village, an' there ain't much passin'. I like to be where I can see passin', an' get out to meetin' easy if it's bad weather. I've been thinkin' — I didn't know but maybe you'd like to have me — I heard you had some trouble with your hands, an' your niece wa'n't well — that I might be willin' to come an' stay three or four weeks. I shouldn't want to promise to stay very long."

"I ain't never been in the habit of keepin' help," returned Mrs. Field. "I've always done my own work."

The other woman's face flushed deeply; she moved toward the door. "I don't know as anything was said about keepin' help," said she. "I ain't never considered myself help. There ain't any need of my goin' out to live. I've got enough to live on, an' I've got good clothes. I've got a black silk stiff enough to stand alone; cost three dollars a yard. I paid seven dollars to have it made up, and the lace on it cost a dollar a yard. I ain't obliged to be at anybody's beck and call."

"I hope I ain't said anything to hurt your feelin's," said Mrs. Field, following her into the entry. "I've always done my own work, an' —"

"We won't speak of it again," said Mrs. Jay. "I'll bid you good-mornin', Mis' Maxwell." Her voice shook, she held up her black skirt, and never looked around as she went down the steps.

Mrs. Field returned to the kitchen. Lois sat beside the window, her head leaning against the sash, looking out. Her mother took some biscuits out of the stove oven and set them on the table with the coffee. "Breakfast is ready," said she.

She sat down at the table. Lois never stirred.

"You needn't worry," said Mrs. Field, in a sarcastic voice; "everything on this table is bought with your own money. I went out last night and got some flour. There's a whole barrelful in the buttery, but I didn't touch it."

Lois drew her chair up to the table, and ate a biscuit and drank a cup of coffee without saying a word. Her eyes were set straight ahead; all her pale features seemed to point out sharply; her whole face had the look of a wedge that could pierce fate. After breakfast she went out of the room, and returned shortly with her hat on.

"Mother," said she.

"What is it?"

"You'd better know what I'm going to do."

"What are you goin' to do?"

"I'm goin' down to that lawyer's office, and — tell him." Lois turned toward the door.

"I s'pose you know all you're goin' to do," said her mother, in a hard voice.

"I'm going to tell the truth," returned Lois, fiercely.

"You're goin' to put your mother in State's prison."

Lois stopped. "Mother, you can't make me believe that."

"It's true, whether you believe it or not. I don't know anything about law, but I'm sure enough of that."

Lois stood looking at her mother. "Then I'll put you there," said she, in a cruel voice. "That's where you ought to go, mother."

She went out of the room, and shut the door hard behind her; then she kept on through the house to the front porch, and sat down. She sat there all the morning, huddled up against a pillar. Her mother worked about the house; Lois could hear her now and then, and every time she shuddered. She had a feeling that the woman in the house was not her mother. Had she been familiar with the vampire superstition, she might have thought of that, and had a fancy that some fiend animated the sober, rigid body of the old New England woman with evil and abnormal life.

At noon Lois went in and ate some dinner mechanically; then she returned. Presently, as she sat there, a bell began tolling, and a funeral procession passed along the road below. Lois watched it listlessly — the black-draped hearse, the slow-marching bearers, the close-covered wagons, and the nodding horses. She could see it plainly through the thin spring branches. It was quite a long procession; she watched it until it passed. The cemetery was only a little way below the house, on the same side of the street. By twisting her head a little, she could have seen the black throng at the gate.

After a while the hearse and the carriages went past on their homeward road at a lively pace, the gate clicked, and Mrs. Jane Maxwell and a young man came up the walk.

Lois stood up shrinkingly as they approached, the door behind her opened, and she heard her mother's voice.

"Good-afternoon," said Mrs. Field, with rigid ceremony, her mouth widened in a smile.

"Good-afternoon, Esther," returned Mrs. Maxwell. "I've been to the funeral, an' I thought I'd jest run in a minute on my way home. I wanted to ask you an' your niece to come over an' take tea to-morrow. Flora, she'd come, but she didn't get out to the funeral. This is my nephew, Francis Arms, my sister's son. I s'pose you remember him when he was a little boy."

Mrs. Field bowed primly to the young man. The old lady was eying Lois. "I s'pose this is your niece, Esther? I heard she'd come," she said, with sharp graciousness.

"This is Miss Lois Field; I'll make you acquainted, Mis' Maxwell," replied Mrs. Field.

Mrs. Maxwell reached out her hand, and Lois took it trembling; her little girlish figure drooped before them all.

"She don't look much like you, Esther. I s'pose she takes after her mother," said Mrs. Maxwell.

"I think she rather favors her father's folks," said Mrs. Field.

"I heard she wa'n't very well, but seems to me she looks pretty smart."

"She ain't been well at all," returned Mrs. Field, in a quick, resentful manner.

"Well, I guess she'll pick up here; Elliot's a real healthy place. She must come over and see us real often. This is my nephew, Francis Arms, Lois. I shall have to get him to beau you around and show you the sights."

Lois glanced timidly up at the young man, and returned his bow slightly.

"Won't you walk in?" said Mrs. Field.

Lois went into the house with the party; the old lady still held her hand in her black-mitted one.

"I want you and my nephew to get acquainted," she whispered; "he's a real nice young man. I'm goin' to have you an' your aunt come over an' take tea to-morrow."

They all seated themselves in the south front room. Lois sat beside Mrs. Maxwell on the high black sofa; her feet swung clear from the floor. The young man, who was opposite, beside the chimney, glanced now and then kindly across at her.

"Francis didn't have to go to the bank this afternoon," said Mrs. Maxwell. "I don't know as I told you, Esther, but he's cashier in the bank; he's got a real good place. Francis ain't never had anything but a common-school education, but he's always been real smart an' steady. Lawyer Totten's son, that's been through college, wanted the place, but they gave it to Francis. Mr. Perry, whose mother was buried this afternoon, is president of the bank, an' that's why it's shut up. Francis felt as if he'd ought to go to the funeral, an' I told him he'd better come in here with me. I suppose you remember Francis when he was a little boy, Esther?"

"No, I guess I don't."

"Why, I should think you'd be likely to. He lived with me

when you was here. He came right after his father died, an' that was before you came here. He was quite a big boy. I should think you'd remember him. You sure you don't, Esther?"

"Yes, I guess I don't."

"Seems to me it's dreadful queer; I guess your memory ain't as good as mine. I s'pose you're beginnin' to feel kind of wonted here, Esther? It's a pretty big house, but then it ain't as if you hadn't been here before. I s'pose it seems kind of familiar to you, if you ain't seen it for so long; I s'pose it all comes back to you, don't it?"

There was a pause. "No, I'm afraid it don't," said Mrs. Field her pale severe face fronting the other woman. Although fairly started forth in the slough of deceit, she still held up her Puritan skirts arduously.

"It's kind of queer it don't, ain't it?" returned Mrs. Maxwell. "The house ain't been altered any, an' the furniture's jest the same. Thomas, he wouldn't have a thing altered; the carpet in his bedroom is wore threadbare, but he wouldn't get a new one nohow. Mis' Jay, she wanted him to get a new cookin'-stove, but he wouldn't hear to it; much as ever he'd let her have a new broom. And it wa'n't because he was stingy; it was jest because he was kind of set, an' had got into the way of thinkin' nothin' had ought to be changed. It wa'n't never my way; I never believed in hangin' on to old shackly things because you've always had 'em. There ain't no use tryin' to set down tables an' chairs as solid as the everlastin' hills. There was Mis' Perry, she that was buried this afternoon, Mr. Perry's mother, when she came here to live after her husband died, she sold off every stick of her old furniture, an' got the handsomest marble-top set that money could buy for her room. She got some pictures in gilt frames too, and a tapestry carpet, and vases and images for her mantel-shelf. She said folks could talk about associations all they wanted to, she hadn't no associations with a lot of old worm-eaten furniture; she'd rather have some that was clean an' new. H'm, anybody to hear folks talk sometimes would think they were blood-relations to old secretaries and bureaus."

Mrs. Maxwell screwed her face contemptuously, as if the talking folk were before her, and there was a pause. The young man looked across at Lois, then turned to her mother, as if about to speak, but his aunt interposed.

"Esther," said she, "I jest wanted to ask you if there wa'n't two of them old swell-front bureaus in the north chamber upstairs."

"I guess there is," replied Mrs. Field. She sat leaning forward toward her callers, with her face fairly strained into hospitable attention.

"Well, I wanted to know. I ain't come beggin', an' I'd 'nough sight rather have a good clean new one, but I'm kind of short of bureau drawers, an' I'd kind of like to have it because 'twas Thomas'. I wonder if you wouldn't jest as soon I'd have one of them bureaus?"

Mrs. Field's face gleamed suddenly. "You can have it jest as well as not," said she.

"Well, there's another thing. I kind of hate to speak about it. Flora said I shouldn't; but I said I would, whether or no. I know you'd rather I would. There's a set of blue china dishes that Nancy, that's Thomas' wife, you know, always said Flora should have when she got done with them. Thomas, he never said anything about it after Nancy died. I didn't know but he might make mention of it in the will. But we all know how that was. I ain't findin' no fault, an' I ain't begrudgin' anything."

"You can have the dishes jest as well as not," returned Mrs. Field, eagerly.

"Well, I didn't know as you'd value them much. I s'posed you'd rather get some new ones. You can get real handsome ones now for ten dollars. Silsbee's got an elegant set in his window. Of course folks that can afford them would rather have them. But I s'pose Flora would think considerable of that old set because it belonged to her aunt Nancy. There's one or two other things I was thinkin' of, but it don't matter about those to-day. It's a beautiful day, ain't it?"

"What be they?" asked Mrs. Field. "If there's anything you want, you're welcome to it."

Mrs. Maxwell glanced at her nephew. He was looking out of the window, with his forehead knitted and his lips compressed. Lois had just thought how cross he looked. "You ain't been out to see anything of the town, have you, Lois?" asked Mrs. Maxwell, sweetly.

Lois started. "No, ma'am," she said, faintly.

"You ain't been into the graveyard, I s'pose?"

"No, ma'am."

"You'd ought to go in there an' see the Mason monument. Francis, don't you want to go over there with her an' show her the Mason monument?"

Francis rose promptly.

"I guess I'd rather not," Lois said, hurriedly.

"Oh, you run right along!" cried Mrs. Maxwell. "You'll want

to see the flowers on Mis' Perry's grave, too. I never saw such handsome flowers as they had, an' they carried them all to the grave. Get your hat, and run right along, it'll do you good."

"You'd better," said the young man, smiling pleasantly down at Lois.

She got up and left the room, and presently returned with her hat on.

"Don't sit down on the damp ground," Mrs. Field said as the two went out. And her voice sounded more like herself than it had done since she left Green River.

Lois walked gravely down the street beside Francis Arms. She had never had any masculine attention. This was the first time she had ever walked alone with a young man. She was full of that shy consciousness which comes to a young girl who has had more dreams than lovers, but her steady, sober face quite concealed it.

Francis kept glancing down at her, trying to think of something to say. She never looked at him, and kept her shabby little shoes pointed straight ahead on the extreme inside of the walk, as intently as if she were walking on a line. Nobody would have dreamed how her heart, in spite of the terrible exigency in which she was placed, was panting insensibly with the sweet rhythm of youth. In the midst of all this trouble and bewilderment, she had not been able to help a strange feeling when she first looked into this young man's face. It was as if she were suddenly thrust off her old familiar places, like a young bird from its nest into space, and had to use a strange new motion of her soul to keep herself from falling.

But Francis guessed nothing of this. "It's a pleasant day," he remarked as they walked along.

"Yes, sir," she replied.

The graveyard gates had been left open after the funeral. They entered, and passed up the driveway along the wheel ruts of the funeral procession. Pink garlands of flowering-almond arched over the old graves, and bushes of bridal-wreath sent out white spikes. Weeping-willows swept over them in lines of gold-green light, and evergreen trees stood among them as they had stood all winter. In many of these were sunken vases and bottles of spring flowers, lilacs and violets.

Lois and Francis Arms went on to the Mason monument.

"This is the one Aunt Jane was speaking about," he said, in a deferential tone.

Lois looked up at the four white marble women grouped around the central shaft, their Greek faces outlined against the

New England sky.

"It was made by a famous sculptor," said Francis; "and it cost a great deal of money."

Lois nodded.

"They box it up in the winter, so it won't be injured by the weather," said Francis.

Lois nodded again. Presently they turned away, and went on to a new grave, covered with wreaths and floral devices. The fragrance of tuberoses and carnations came in their faces.

"This is the grave Aunt Jane wanted you to see," said Francis.

"Yes, sir," returned Lois.

They stood staring silently at the long mound covered with flowers. Francis turned.

"Suppose we go over this way," said he.

Lois followed him as he strode along the little grassy paths between the burial lots. On the farther side of the cemetery the ground sloped abruptly to a field of new grass. Francis stooped and felt of the short grass on the bank.

"It's dry," said he. "I don't think your aunt would mind. Suppose we sit down here and rest a few minutes?"

Lois looked at him hesitatingly.

"Oh, sit down just a few minutes," he said, with a pleasant laugh.

They both seated themselves on the bank, and looked down into the field.

"It's pleasant here, isn't it?" said Francis.

"Real pleasant."

The young man looked kindly, although a little constrainedly, down into his companion's face.

"I hear you haven't been very well," said he. "I hope you feel better since you came to Elliot?"

"Yes, thank you; I guess I do," replied Lois.

Francis still looked at her. Her little face bent, faintly rosy, under her hat. There was a grave pitifulness, like an old woman's, about her mouth, but her shoulders looked very young and slender.

"Suppose you take off your hat," said he, "and let the air come on your forehead. I've got mine off; it's more comfortable. You won't catch cold. It's warm as summer."

Lois took off her hat.

"That's better," said Francis, approvingly. "You're going to live right along here in Elliot with your aunt, aren't you?"

Lois looked up at him suddenly. She was very pale, and her

eyes were full of terror.

"Why, what is the matter? What have I said?" he cried out, in bewilderment.

Lois bent over and hid her face; her back heaved with sobs.

Francis stared at her. "Why, what is the matter?" he cried again. "Have I done anything?" He hesitated. Then he put his hand on her little moist curly head. Lois' hair was not thick, but it curled softly. "Why, you poor little girl," said he; "don't cry so;" and his voice was full of embarrassed tenderness.

Lois sobbed harder.

"Now, see here," said Francis. "I haven't known you more than an hour, and I don't know what the matter is, and I don't know but you'll think I'm officious, but I'll do anything in the world to help you, if you'll only tell me."

Lois shook off his hand and sat up. "It isn't anything," said she, catching her breath, and setting her tear-stained face defiantly ahead.

"Don't you feel well?"

Lois nodded vaguely, keeping her quivering mouth firmly set. They were both silent for a moment, then Lois spoke without looking at him.

"Do you know if there's any school here that I could get?" said she.

"A school?"

"Yes. I want to get a chance to teach. I've been teaching, but I've lost my school."

"And you want to get one here?"

"Yes. Do you know of any?"

"Why, see here," said Francis. "It's none of my business, but I thought you hadn't been very well. Why don't you take a little vacation?"

"I can't," returned Lois, in a desperate tone. "I've got to do something."

"Why, won't your aunt —" He stopped short. The conviction that the stern old woman who had inherited the Maxwell property was too hard and close to support her little delicate orphan niece seized upon him. Lois' next words strengthened it.

"I lost my school," she went on, still keeping her face turned toward the meadow and speaking fast. "Ida Starr got it away from me. Her father is school-committee-man, and he said he didn't think I was able to teach, just because he brought me home in his buggy one day when I was a little faint. I had a note from him that morning mother — that morning she came down here. I was just going to school, and I was a good deal better, when Mr. Starr's boy brought it. He said he thought it was better for me to take a little vacation. I knew what that meant. I knew Ida had wanted the school right along. I told Amanda I was coming down here. She tried to stop me, but I had money enough. Mr. Starr sent me what was owing to me, and I came. I thought I might just as well. I thought mother — Amanda was dreadfully scared, but I told her I was going to come. I can't go back to Green River; I haven't got money enough." Lois's voice broke; she hid her face again.

"Oh, don't feel so," cried Francis. "You don't want to go back to Green River."

"Yes, I do. I want to get back. It's awful here, awful. I never knew anything so awful."

Francis stared at her pityingly. "Why, you poor little girl, are you as homesick as that?" he said.

Lois only sobbed in answer.

"Look here!" said Francis — he leaned over her, and his voice sank to a whisper — "it's none of my business, but I think you'd better tell me; it won't go any further — isn't your aunt good to you? Doesn't she treat you well?"

Lois shook her head vaguely. "I can't go back anyway," she moaned. "Ida's got my school. I haven't got anything to do there. Don't you think I can get a school here?"

"I am afraid you can't," said Francis. "You see, the schools have all begun now. But you mustn't feel so bad. Don't." He touched her shoulder gently. "Poor little girl!" said he. "Perhaps I ought not to speak so to you, but you make me so sorry for you I can't help it. Now you must cheer up; you'll get along all right. You won't be homesick a bit after a little while; you'll like it here. There are some nice girls about your age. My cousin Flora will come and see you. She's older than you, but she's a real nice girl. She's feeling rather upset over something now, too. Now come, let's get up and go and see some more of the monuments. You don't want a school. Your aunt can lookout for you. I should laugh if she couldn't. She's a rich woman, and you're all she's got in the world. Now come, let's cheer up, and go look at some more grave-stones."

"I guess I'd rather go home," said Lois, faintly.

"Too tired? Well, let's sit here a little while longer, then. You mustn't go home with your eyes red, your aunt will think I've been scolding you."

Francis looked down at her with smiling gentleness. He was a handsome young man with a pale straight profile, his face was very steady and grave when he was not animated, and his smile occasioned a certain pleasant surprise. He was tall, and there was a boyish clumsiness about his shoulders in his gray coat. He reached out with a sudden impulse, and took Lois' little thin hand in his own with a warm clasp.

"Now cheer up," said he. "See how pleasant it looks down in the field."

They sat looking out over the field; the horizon sky stretched out infinitely in straight blue lines; one could imagine he saw it melt into the sea which lay beyond; the field itself, with its smooth level of young grass, was like a waveless green sea. A white road lay on the left, and a man was walking on it with a weary, halting gait; he carried a tin dinner-pail, which dipped and caught the western sunlight at every step. A cow lowed, and a pair of white horns tossed over some bars at the right of the field; a boy crossed it with long, loping strides and preliminary swishes of a birch stick. Then a whistle blew with a hoarse musical note, and a bell struck six times.

Lois freed her hand and got up. "I guess I must go," said she. Her cheeks were blushing softly as she put on her hat.

"Well, I should like to sit here an hour longer, but maybe your aunt will think it's growing damp for you to be out-of-doors," said Francis, standing up.

As they went between the graves, he caught her hand again, and led her softly along. When they reached the gate, he dropped it with a kindly pressure.

"Now remember, you are going to cheer up," he said, "and you're going to have real nice times here in Elliot." When they reached the Maxwell house, his aunt was coming down the walk.

"Oh, there you are!" she called out. "I was jest goin' home. Well, what did you think of the Mason monument, Lois?"

"It's real handsome."

"Ain't it handsome? An' wa'n't the flowers on Mis' Perry's grave elegant? Good-night. I'm goin' to have you an' your aunt come over an' take tea to-morrow, an' then you can get acquainted with Flora."

"Good-night," said Francis, smiling, and the aunt and nephew went on down the road. She carried something bulky under her shawl, and she walked with a curious side-wise motion, keeping the side next her nephew well forward.

"Don't you want me to carry your bundle, Aunt Jane?" Lois heard him say as they walked off.

"No," the old woman replied, hastily and peremptorily. "It

ain't anything."

When Lois went into the house, her mother gave her a curious look of stern defiance and anxiety. She saw that her eyes were red, as if she had been crying, but she said nothing, and went about getting tea.

After tea the minister and his wife called. Green River was a conservative little New England village; it had always been the custom there when the minister called to invite him to offer a prayer. Mrs. Field felt it incumbent upon her now; if she had any reluctance, she did not yield to it. Just before the callers left she said, with the conventional solemn drop of the voice, "Mr. Wheeler, won't you offer a prayer before you go?"

The minister was an elderly man with a dull benignity of manner; he had not said much; his wife, who was portly and full of gracious volubility, had done most of the talking. Now she immediately sank down upon her knees with a wide flare of her skirts, and her husband then twisted himself out of his chair, clearing his throat impressively. Mrs. Field stood up, and got down on her stiff knees with an effort. Lois slid down from the sofa and went out of the room. She stole through her mother's into her own bedroom, and locked herself in as usual, then she lay down on her bed. She could hear the low rumble of the minister's voice for some time; then it ceased. She heard the chairs pushed back; then the minister's wife's voice in the gracious crescendo of parting; then the closing of the front door. Shortly afterward she heard a door open, and another voice, which she recognized as Mrs. Maxwell's. The voice talked on and on; once in a while she heard her mother's in brief reply. It grew dark; presently she heard heavy shuffling steps on the stairs; something knocked violently against the wall; the side door, which was near her room, was opened. Lois got up and peered out of the window; her mother and Mrs. Maxwell went slowly and painfully down the driveway, carrying a bureau between them.

CHAPTER VI

Mrs. Maxwell had invited Mrs. Field and Lois to take tea with her the next afternoon, and had hinted there might be other company. "There's a good many I should like to ask," she had said, "but I ain't situated so I can jest now, an' it's a dreadful puzzle to know who to leave out without offendin' them. I'm goin' to have the minister an' his wife anyhow, an' Lawyer Tuxbury an' his sister. I should ask Flora, but if she comes the children have got to, an' I can't have them anyhow; they're the worst-actin' young ones at the table I ever saw in my life. There's two or three men I'm goin' to ask. Now you an' Lois come real early, Esther."

Mrs. Field's ideas of early, when invited to spend the afternoon and take tea, were primitive. Directly after the dinner dishes were put away, about one o'clock, she spoke to Lois in the harsh, defiant tone she now used toward her. "You'd better go an' get ready," said she. "She wanted us to come early."

A stubborn look came into Lois's face. "I ain't going," said she, in an undertone.

"What did you say?"

"I ain't going."

"Then you can stay to home, if you want to get your mother into trouble an' make folks think we're guilty of somethin'."

Mrs. Field went into her bedroom to get ready. Presently Lois went softly through on her way to her own. Jane Field stood before her little mirror, brushed her gray hair in smooth curves around her ears, and pinned her black woollen dress with a gold-rimmed brooch containing her dead sister's and her husband's hair.

Lois, before her own glass, twisted up her pretty hair carefully; she pulled a few curly locks loose on her temples, thinking half indignantly and shamefacedly how she should see that young man again. Lois was bewildered and terrified, borne down by reflected guilt, almost as if it were her own. She had a wild dread of this going out to tea, meeting more strangers, and seeing her mother act out a further lie; but she could not help being a young girl, and arranging those little locks on her forehead for Francis Arms to see.

When she and her mother stepped out of the door, a strong wind came in their faces.

"Wait a minute," said Mrs. Field. She went back into the house and got Lois's sack. "Put this on," said she.

And Lois put it on.

The wind was from the east, and had the salt smell of the sea. All the white-flowering bushes in the yards and the fruit trees bowed toward the west. There was a storm of white petals. Lois, as she and her mother walked against the wind, kept putting her hand to her hair, to keep it in place.

Mrs. Maxwell's house was a large cottage with a steep Gothic roof jutting over a piazza on each side. The house was an old one, and originally very simple in its design; but there had been evidently at some time a flood-tide of prosperity in the fortunes of its owner, which had left marks in various improvements. There was a large ornate bay-window in front, which contrasted oddly with the severe white peak of wall above it; the piazzas had railings in elaborate scroll-work; and the windows were set with four large panes of glass, instead of the original twelve small ones. The front yard was inclosed by a fine iron fence. But the highest mark was shown by a little white marble statue in the midst of it. There was no other in the village outside of the cemetery. Mrs. Jane Maxwell's house was always described to inquiring strangers as the one with the statue in front of it.

Lois, as they went up the walk, looked wonderingly at this marble girl standing straight and white in the midst of a votive circle of box. The walk, too, was bordered with box, and there was a strange pungent odor from it.

Mrs. Field rang the door-bell, and she and Lois stood waiting. Nobody came.

Mrs. Field rang again and again. "I'm goin' round to the other door," she announced finally. "Mebbe they don't use this one."

Lois followed her mother around to the other side of the house to the door opening on the south piazza. Mrs. Field rang again, and they waited: then she gave a harder pull. A voice sounded unexpectedly close to them from behind the blinds of a window:

"You jest walk right in," said the voice, which was at once flurried and ceremonious. "Open the door an' go right in, an' turn to the right, an' set down in the parlor. I'll be in in jest a minute. I ain't quite dressed."

Lois and her mother went in as they were directed, and sat down in two of the parlor chairs. The room looked very grand to Mrs. Field. She stared at the red velvet furniture, the tapestry carpet, and the long lace curtains, and thought, with a hardening heart, how, at all events, she was not defrauding this other woman of a fine parlor. It was to her mind much more splendid than the sitting-room in the other house, with its dim old-fashioned state, and even than the great north parlor, whose furniture and paper had been imported from England at great cost nearly a hundred years ago.

Mrs. Maxwell did not appear for a half-hour. Now and then they heard a scurry of feet, the rattle of dishes, and the closing of a door. They sat primly waiting. They had not removed their wraps. Lois looked very pale against the red back of her chair.

"Don't you feel well?" asked her mother.

"Yes, I feel well enough," replied Lois.

"You look sick enough," said her mother harshly.

Lois looked out of the window at the marble girl in the yard, and her mouth quivered.

Presently Mrs. Maxwell came, in her soft flurry of silk and old ribbons. She had on a black lace head-dress trimmed with purple flowers, and she wore her black kid gloves.

"I'm real sorry I had to keep you waitin' so long, Esther," said she; "but we were kinder late about dinner. Do take off your things. Flora she'll be down in a few minutes; she's jest gone upstairs to change her dress an' comb her hair. It's a beautiful day, ain't it?"

The three settled themselves in the parlor. Lois sat beside the window, her hands folded meekly in her lap; her mother and Mrs. Maxwell knitted.

"Don't you do any fancy-work, Lois?" asked Mrs. Maxwell.

"No, she don't do much," replied her mother for her.

"Don't she? I'd like to know! Now Flora, she does considerable. She's makin' a real handsome tidy now. She'll show you how, Lois, if you'd like to make one. It's real easy an' it don't cost a great deal — but then cost ain't much object to you." Mrs. Maxwell laughed an unpleasant snigger. Then she resumed: "Some tidies would look real handsome on some of them great bare chairs over to your house; there ain't one there so far as I know. Thomas he wouldn't never have a new thing in the house; he was terrible set and notional about it and he was terrible tight with his money. I don't care if I do say it; everybody knows it; an' I don't see why it's any worse to say things that's true about the dead than the livin'. With some folks it's all 'Oh, don't say nothin'; he's dead. Cover it all up; he's buried an' bury it too, an' set all the roses an' pinks a-growin' over it.' I tell you sometimes nettles will sprout, an' when they do, it don't make it any better to call 'em pinks. Thomas Maxwell was terrible tight. I ain't forgot how he talked because we bought this parlor furniture and put big lights in the windows, an' had that iron fence. Then my poor husband had gone into business with your husband, an' they seemed to be making money. Why shouldn't he have bought a few things we'd always done without, I'd like to know? You remember what a time the old man made when we bought these things, Esther, I suppose?"

"I can't say as I do," returned Mrs. Field.

"Why, seems to me it's funny you don't. You sure?"

Mrs. Field nodded.

"Well, it's queer you don't. He made an awful time over it; but the worst of it was over that image out in the yard. I b'lieve he always thought my poor husband and yours failed up because we bought that image. There was one thing about it, your husband wa'n't never extravagant, though, was he? Thomas Maxwell couldn't say his son wasted his money, whatever else he said. Your husband was always prudent, wa'n't he, Esther?"

"Yes, I always thought Edward Maxwell was prudent," returned Mrs. Field.

Lois, staring soberly and miserably out of the window, saw just then a stout girlish figure, leant to one side with the weight of a valise, pass hurriedly out of the yard. She wondered if it was Flora Maxwell, and watched the pink flowers in her hat and the blue folds of her dress out of sight down the street.

"I guess your husband took after his father a little; I guess he was a little savin'," said Mrs. Maxwell. "I know Edward looked kind of scared when he came over one night an' saw that image just after we'd got it set up, an' he asked how much it cost. It did cost considerable. We didn't ever tell anybody just how much; but I didn't care; I'd always wanted one; an' I made up my mind I'd rather have that if I had to go without some other things. An' my husband wanted it too; he was one of the Maxwells, you know, an' I think they all had a taste for such things if they wa'n't too tight to get 'em. As for me, I had to do without all my young days, an' I have to now except for the few things we got together along then when my poor husband seemed to be prospering; but I've always been crazy over images, an' I've always thought one in a front yard was about the most ornamental thing anybody could have. I've told Flora a good many times that I believed if I'd had advantages when I was young, I should have made images. Don't you think that one's handsome, Esther?"

"Real handsome," said Mrs. Field.

"Some folks have found fault with it because it didn't have more clothes on, but it ain't as if it was in a cemetery. Of course it would have to be dressed different if it was. An' it ain't anything but marble, when you come right down to it. I think there's such a thing as bein' too particular, for my part, don't you?"

"Yes, I do," replied Mrs. Field, looking out at the marble figure.

"Well, I do. Mis' Jay said, after my husband died, that she should think I'd like to put up that image for a kind of monument for him. I didn't feel as if I could put up anything more than stones; but I did think a little of it, and I knew if I did, I should have to have some wings made on it, and a cape or a shawl over the neck and arms; but out here it's different. I look out at it a good many times, an' I'm thankful it ain't got any more on, clothes do get so out of fashion. You know how they look in photographs sometimes. I s'pose that's the reason that the men who make these images don't put any more on. There! I must show you my photograph album, Esther."

Mrs. Maxwell took a heavy album with gilt clasps from the centre-table, and drew a chair close to Mrs. Field.

"Now you get a chair, an' come on the other side, Lois," said she, "an' I can show 'em to both of you."

Lois obeyed, and Mrs. Maxwell turned over the album leaves and explained the pictures.

"This is a lady I used to know," said she. "She lived in North Elliot. She's dead now. That's her husband; he's married again. His second wife's kind of silly. Ain't much like the first one. She was a real stepper. That's Flora Lowe's baby — the first one — an' that's Flora. I think it flatters her. That's my Flora. It ain't very good. She looks terrible sober. There's my poor husband. I s'pose you remember him, Esther? Of course you know how he used to look. Do you think it's a good likeness?"

"I don't know. I guess it's pretty good, ain't it?" stammered Mrs. Field.

"Well, some think it is, and some don't. I ain't never liked it very well myself, but it was all I had. It was taken some years before he died. I guess jest about the time you was down here. There! I s'pose you know whose this is?"

It was her own photograph that Mrs. Field leant over and saw, and Lois on the other side saw it also.

"Yes, I guess I do," she said.

"Was it a pretty good one of your sister?"

There was a strange gulping sound in Mrs. Field's throat. She did not answer. Mrs. Maxwell thought she did not hear, and repeated her question.

"No, I don't think 'twas, very," said Mrs. Field hoarsely.

"Well, of course I don't know. I never see her. You remember you gave this to me when you was here. I always thought you must look alike, judging from your pictures. I never see pictures so much alike in my life. I don't know how many folks have thought they were taken for the same person, an' I've always thought so too. If anything your sister's picture looks more like you than your own does; but I've always told which was which by that breast-pin in your sister's. Why, you've got on that breast-pin now, ain't you, Esther?"

"Yes, I have," said Mrs. Field.

"I s'pose your sister left it to you. Well, Lois wouldn't want to wear it as I know of. It's rather old for her. Why, Lois, what's the matter?"

Lois had gotten up abruptly. "I guess I'll go over to the window," said she, in a quick trembling voice.

Mrs. Maxwell looked at her sharply. "Why, you're dreadful pale. You ain't faint, are you?"

"No, ma'am."

Mrs. Field turned over another page of the album. Her pale face had a hard, indifferent look. Mrs. Maxwell nudged her, and nodded toward Lois in the window.

"She looks dreadful," she whispered.

"I don't see as she looks any worse than she's been doin' right along," said Mrs. Field, without lowering her voice. "What baby is this?"

"It's Mis' Robinson's; it's dead. Hadn't I better get her something to take? I've got some currant wine. Maybe a little of that would do her good."

"No, thank you; I don't care for any," Lois interposed quickly.

"Hadn't you better have a little? You look real pale."

"No, thank you."

"Now you needn't mind takin' it, Lois, if you do belong to any temperance society. It wouldn't go to the head of a baby kitten."

"I'm just as much obliged, but I don't care for any," said Lois.

Mrs. Maxwell turned over a page of the album. "That's Mis' Robinson's sister. She's dead too. She married a man over at Milton, an' didn't live a year," she said ostentatiously. "Hadn't I better get her a little?" she whispered.

"Mebbe it would do her good, if you've got it to spare," Mrs. Field whispered back.

"Here's the minister's little boy that died," said Mrs. Maxwell. "He wasn't sick but a day. He ate milk an' cherries. I wonder where Flora is? She didn't have a thing to do but comb her hair and change her dress. I guess I'll go call her."

Mrs. Maxwell's face was frowning with innocent purpose, but there was a sly note in her voice. She hurried out of the room and they heard her call, "Flora! Flora!" in the entry. Then they heard her footsteps on the cellar stairs.

Lois turned to her mother. "Mother," said she, "I can't stand it — I can't stand it anyway in the world."

Her mother turned over another page of the photograph album. She looked at a faded picture of a middle-aged woman, whose severe and melancholy face seemed to have betrayed all the sadness and toil of her whole life to the camera. She noted deliberately the old-fashioned sweep of the skirt quite across the little card, and the obsolete sleeves, then she spoke as if she were talking to the picture: "I'm a-followin' out my own law an' my own right," said she. "I ain't ashamed of it. If you want to be you can."

"It's awful. Oh, mother, don't!"

"A good many things are awful," said her mother. "Injustice is awful; if you want to set yourself up against your mother, you can. I've laid out this road that's just an' right, an' I'm goin' on it; you can do jest as you're a-mind to. If you want to tell her when she comes back, you can. I ain't ashamed of it, for I know I'm doin' what is just an' right."

Mrs. Field noted how the photographed woman's dress was trimmed with fringe, after the fashion of one she had worn twenty years ago.

Lois looked across the room at her mother's pale, stern face bending over the album. The garlands on Mrs. Maxwell's parlor carpet might have been the flora of a whole age, she and her mother seemed so far apart, with that recession of soul which can cover more than earthly spaces. To the young girl with her scared, indignant eyes the older woman seemed actually living and breathing under new conditions in some strange element.

"Flora, Flora, where be you?" Mrs. Maxwell called out in the entry.

They heard her climbing the chamber stairs; but she soon came into the parlor with a little glass of currant wine.

"Here, you'd better drink this right down," she said to Lois; "it won't hurt you. I don't see where Flora is, for my part. She ain't upstairs. Drink it right down."

Lois drank the little glass of wine without any demur. Her mother glanced sharply at the album as she took it.

"I can't imagine where Flora is," said Mrs. Maxwell.

"I saw somebody go out of the yard a while ago," said Lois.

"You did? Was she kind of stout with light hair?"

"Yes, 'm."

"It was Flora then. I don't see where she's gone. Mebbe she went down to the store to get some more thread for her tidy. Now I guess you'll feel better."

"Who's this a picture of?" asked Mrs. Field.

"Hold it up. Oh, that's Mis' John Robbins! She's dead. Yes, I guess Flora must have gone after that thread. She'll show you how to make that tidy, Lois, if you want to learn; it's real handsome. I guess she'll be here before long."

But when Mrs. Maxwell had shown her guests all the photographs in the album and a book of views in Palestine, and it was nearly four o'clock, Flora still had not come.

"Do you see anybody comin'?" Mrs. Maxwell kept asking Lois at the window.

Before Mrs. Maxwell spoke, a nervous vibration seemed to seize upon her whole body. She cleared her throat sharply. It was like a premonitory click of machinery before motion, and Lois waited, numb with fear, for what she might say. Suppose she should suddenly suspect, and should cry out, "Is this woman here Esther Maxwell?"

But all Mrs. Maxwell's thoughts were on her absent daughter. "I don't see where she is," said she. "Here she's got to make cream-tarter biscuits for tea, an' it's 'most time for the folks to come."

"I'm afraid we came too early," said Mrs. Field.

"Oh, no, you didn't," returned Mrs. Maxwell politely. "It ain't half as pleasant goin' as late as they do here when they're asked out to tea. You don't see anything of 'em; they begin to eat jest as soon as they come, an' it seems as if that was all they come for. The old-fashioned way of goin' right after dinner, an' takin' your sewin's, a good deal better, accordin' to my way of thinkin', but they ain't done so for years here. Elliot is a pretty fashionable place. I s'pose it must be very different up in Green River, where you come from?"

"Yes, I guess 'tis," said Mrs. Field.

The front gate clicked, and Mrs. Maxwell peered cautiously around a lace curtain. Two ladies in their best black dresses came up the walk, stepping with a pleasant ceremony.

"There's Mis' Isaac Robbins an' Ann 'Liza White," Mrs. Maxwell whispered agitatedly. "I shall have to go right out in the kitchen an' make them biscuits the minute they get here. I don't see what Flora Maxwell is thinkin' of."

Mrs. Maxwell greeted her friends at the door with a dignified

bustle, showed them into her bedroom to lay aside their bonnets;
then she introduced them to Mrs. Field and Lois in the parlor.

"There!" said she; "now I've got to let you entertain each
other a few minutes. I've got something to see to. Flora she's
stepped out, an' I guess she's forgot how late 'tis."

After Mrs. Maxwell had left the room, the guests sat around
with a kind of solemn primness as if they were in meeting; they
seemed almost hostile. The elder of the new-comers took out her
knitting, and fell to work. She was a tall, pale, severely wrinkled
woman, and a ruffled trimming on her dress gave her high shoulders a curiously girlish air. Finally the woman who had come with
her asked pantingly how Mrs. Field liked Elliot, and if she thought
it changed much. The color flashed over her little face, with its
softly scalloping profile, as she spoke. Her hair was crimped in
even waves. She wore nice white ruching in her neck and sleeves,
and flat satin folds crossed each other exactly over her flat chest.
Her nervous self-consciousness did not ruffle her fine order, and
she did not smile as she spoke.

"I like it pretty well," replied Mrs. Field. "I dunno as I can tell
whether it's changed much or not." She knitted fast.

"The meetin'-house has been made over since you was here,"
volunteered the elder woman. She did not look up from her knitting.

Presently Lois, at the window, saw Mr. Tuxbury's sister, Mrs.
Lowe, coming, and the minister's wife, hurrying with a volumi-
nous swing of her skirts, in her wake. The minister's wife had been
calling, but Mrs. Lowe, who was a little deaf, had not heard her,
and it was not until she shut the iron gate almost in her face that
she saw her. Then the two came up the walk together. Lois
watched them. The coming of all these people was to her like the
closing in of a crowd of witnesses, and for her guilt instead of her
mother's. The minister's wife looked up and nodded graciously to
her, setting the bunch of red and white cherries on her bonnet
trembling. Lois inclined her pale young face soberly in response.

"That girl looks sick," said the minister's wife to Mrs. Lowe.

There was no more silence and primness after the minister's
wife entered. Her florid face beamed on them all with masterly
smiles. She put the glasses fastened to her high satin bosom with a
gold chain to her eyes, and began sewing on a white apron. "I
meant to have come before," said she, "and brought my sewing
and had a real sociable time, but one thing after another has
delayed me; and I don't know when Mr. Wheeler will get here; I
left him with a caller. But we have been delayed very pleasantly in

one respect;" she looked smilingly and significantly at Mrs. Maxwell.

All the other ladies stared. Mrs. Maxwell, standing in their midst, with a large cambric apron over her dress, and a powder of flour on one cheek, looked wonderingly back at the minister's wife.

"I suppose you all know what I mean?" said Mrs. Wheeler, still smiling. "I suppose Mrs. Maxwell has not kept the glad tidings to herself." In spite of her smiling face, there was a slight doubt and hesitancy in her manner.

Mrs. Maxwell's old face suddenly paled, and at the same time grew alert. Her black eyes, on Mrs. Wheeler's face, were sharply bright.

"Mebbe I have, an' mebbe I ain't," said she, and she smiled too.

"Well," said the minister's wife, "I told Flora that her mother must be a brave woman to invite company to tea the afternoon her daughter was married, and I thought we all ought to appreciate it."

The other women gasped. Mrs. Maxwell's face was yellow-white in its framework of curls; there was a curious noise in her throat, like a premonitory click of a clock before striking.

"Well," said she, "Flora'd had this day set for the weddin' for six months. When her uncle died, we talked a little about puttin' of it off, but she thought 'twas a bad sign. So it seemed best for her to get married without any fuss at all about it. An' I thought if I had a little company to tea, it would do as well as a weddin'."

Mrs. Maxwell's old black eyes travelled slowly and unflinchingly around the company, resting on each in turn as if she had with each a bout of single combat. The other women's eyes were full of scared questionings as they met hers.

"They got off in the three-o'clock train," remarked the minister's wife, trying to speak easily.

"That was the one they'd talked of," said Mrs. Maxwell calmly. "Now I guess I shall have to leave you ladies to entertain each other a few minutes."

When Mrs. Maxwell had left the room, the ladies stared at each other.

"Do you s'pose she didn't know about it?" whispered Mrs. Lowe.

"I don't know," whispered the minister's wife. "I was very much afraid she didn't at first. I began to feel very nervous. I knew Mr. Wheeler would have been much distressed if he had suspected anything clandestine."

"Did she have a new dress?" asked Mrs. Robbins.

"No," replied the minister's wife; "and that was one thing that made me suspicious. She wore her old blue one, but George Freeman wore a nice new suit."

"I heard," said Mrs. Lowe, "that Flora had all her underclothes made before old Mr. Maxwell died, an' she hadn't got any of her dresses. I had it pretty straight. She told my Flora."

"I had heard that the wedding was postponed on account of Mr. Maxwell's death, and so I was a little surprised when Mr. Wheeler came to me and said they were in the parlor to be married," said the minister's wife; "but I put on my dress as quick as I could, and went in to witness it."

"How did Flora appear?" asked Mrs. Lowe.

"Well, I thought she looked rather sober, but I don't know as she looked any more so than girls usually do when they're married. I have seen them come to the parsonage looking more as if they were going to their own funerals than their weddings, they were so scared and quiet and sober. Now Flora —" The minister's wife stopped short, she heard Mrs. Maxwell coming and she turned the conversation with a jolt of conscience into another channel. "Yes, it is very dry," said she effusively; "we need rain very much indeed."

The little woman with the crimped hair colored very painfully.

Mrs. Maxwell made frequent errands into the room, and her daughter's wedding had to be discussed guardedly. Always after she went out, the women looked at each other in an agony of inquiry.

"Do you s'pose she knew?" they whispered.

Mrs. Field said nothing; she sat grimly quiet, knitting. Lois looked silently out of the window. Both of them knew that Mrs. Maxwell had not known of her daughter's wedding. Presently a man's voice could be heard out in the kitchen.

"It's Francis," said Mrs. Lowe. "I wonder if he knew?"

Lois started, and blushed softly, but nobody noticed her.

There was a deep silence in the parlor; the women were listening to the hum of voices in the kitchen.

"Don't you think it's dreadful close here?" said Mrs. Lowe.

"Yes, I think it is," assented the minister's wife.

"I think it would be a good plan to open the door a little ways," said Mrs. Lowe, and she opened it cautiously.

Still they could distinguish nothing from the hum of voices out in the kitchen.

Mrs. Maxwell was in reality speaking low lest they should hear, although she was clutching her nephew's arm hard, and the veins in her thin temples and her throat were swelling purple. When he had entered she had sprung at him. "Did you hear about it? I want to know if you knew about it," said she, grasping his arm with her wiry fingers, as if she were trying to wreak her anger on him.

"Knew about what?" said Francis wonderingly. "What is the matter, Aunt Jane?"

"Did you know Flora went to the minister's and got married this afternoon?"

"No," said Francis slowly, "I didn't; but I knew she would, well enough."

"Did Flora tell you?"

"No, she didn't tell me, but I knew she wouldn't do anything else."

"Knew she wouldn't do anything else? I'd like to know what you're talkin' about, Francis Arms."

"I knew as long as she was Flora Maxwell, and her wedding was set for to-day three months ago, it wasn't very likely that old Mr. Maxwell's dying and not leaving her his money, and your not liking it, was going to stop her."

"Hadn't it ought to have stopped her? Hadn't the wishes of a mother that's slaved for her all her life, and didn't want her to get married without a silk gown to her back to a man that ain't any prospects of being able to buy her any, ought to have stopped her, I'd like to know?"

"I guess Flora didn't think much about silk gowns, Aunt Jane," said Francis, and his face reddened a little. "I guess she didn't think much about anything but George."

"George! What's George Freeman? What's all the Freemans? I ain't never liked them. They wa'n't never up to our folks. His mother ain't never had a black silk dress to her name — never had a thing better than black cashmere, an' they ain't never had a thing but oil-cloth in their front entry, an' the Perry's ain't never noticed them either. I ain't never wanted Flora to go into that family. I never felt as if she was lookin' high enough, an' I knew George couldn't get no kind of a livin' jest being clerk in Mason's store. But I felt different about it before Thomas died, for I thought she'd have money enough of her own, an' she was gettin' a little on in years, and George was good-lookin' enough. After Thomas died an' left all his money to Edward's wife, I hadn't an idea Flora would be such a fool as to think of marryin' George

Freeman. She'd been better off if she'd never been married. I thought she'd given up all notions of it."

"Well, don't you worry, Aunt Jane," said Francis in a hearty voice. "Make the best of it. I guess they'll get along all right. If George can't buy Flora a silk dress I will. I'd have bought her one anyway if I'd known."

"You can stand up for her all you want to, Francis Arms," cried his aunt. "It's nothin' more than I ought to expect. What do you s'pose I'm goin' to do? Here I am with all these folks to tea an' Flora gone. She might have waited till to-morrow. Here they are all pryin' an' suspectin'. But they shan't know if I die for it. They shan't know that good-for-nothin' girl went off an' got married unbeknown to me. They've had enough to crow over because we didn't get Thomas Maxwell's money; they shan't have this nohow. You'll have to lend me some money, an' I'm goin' to Boston to-morrow an' I'm goin' to buy a silk dress for Flora an' get it made, so she can go out bride when she comes home; an' they've got to come here an' board. I might jest as well have the board-money as them Freemans, an' folks shan't think we ain't on good terms. Can you let me have some money to-morrow mornin'?"

"Of course I can, Aunt Jane," said Francis soothingly. "I'll make Flora a wedding-present of it."

"I don't want it for a weddin'-present. I'll pay you back some time. If you're goin' to give her a weddin'-present, I'd rather you'd give her somethin' silver that she can show. I ain't goin' to have you give her clothes for a weddin'-present, as if we was poor as the Freemans. You didn't have any pride. There ain't anybody in this family ever had any pride but me, an' I have to keep it up, an' nobody liftin' a finger to help me. Oh, dear!" the old woman quivered from head to foot. Her face worked as if she was in silent hysterics.

"Don't, Aunt Jane," whispered her nephew — "don't feel so bad. Maybe it's all for the best. Why, what is the matter with your wrist?"

"I burned it takin' the biscuit out of the oven," she groaned.

"Why, it's an awful burn. Don't you want something on it?"

"No, I don't mind no burns."

Suddenly Mrs. Maxwell moved away from her nephew. She began arranging the plates on the table. "You go into the parlor," said she sharply, "an' don't you let 'em know you didn't know about it. You act kind of easy an' natural when they speak about it. You go right in; tea won't be ready quite yet. I've got something a little extra to see about."

Francis went into the parlor and greeted the guests, shaking hands with them rather boyishly and awkwardly. The minister's wife made room for him on the sofa beside her.

"I suppose you'd like to hear about your cousin's wedding that I went to this afternoon," said she, with a blandness that had a covert meaning to the other women, who listened eagerly.

"Yes, I would," replied Francis, with steady gravity.

"I suppose it wasn't such a surprise to you as it was to us?" said she directly, and the other women panted.

"No, I suppose it wasn't," said Francis.

Mrs. Lowe and Mrs. Robbins glanced at each other.

"*He* knew," Mrs. Lowe motioned with her lips, nodding.

"*She* didn't," Mrs. Robbins motioned back, shaking her head.

Francis sat beside the minister's wife. She talked on about the wedding, and he listened soberly and assentingly.

"Well, it will be your turn next, Francis," said she, with a sly graciousness, and the young man reddened, and laughed constrainedly.

Francis seldom glanced at Lois, but it was as if her little figure in the window was all he saw in the room. She seemed so near his consciousness that she shut out all else besides. Lois did not look at him, but once in a while she put up her hand and arranged the hair on her forehead, and after she had done so felt as if she saw herself with his eyes. The air was growing cool; presently Lois coughed.

"You'd better come away from that window," said Mrs. Field, speaking out suddenly.

There was no solicitude in her tone; it was more like harsh command. Everybody looked at Lois; Francis with an anxious interest. He partly arose as if to make room for her on the sofa, but she simply moved her chair farther back. Presently Francis went over and shut the window.

The minister, Mr. Tuxbury, and Mrs. Robbin's husband all arrived together shortly afterward. Mrs. Maxwell announced that tea was ready.

"Will you please walk out to tea?" said she, standing at the door, in a ceremonious hush. And the company arose hesitatingly, looking at one another for precedence, and straggled out.

"You sit here," said Mrs. Maxwell to Lois, and she pointed to a chair beside Francis.

Lois sat down and fixed her eyes upon her green and white plate while the minister asked the blessing.

"It's a pleasant day, isn't it?" said Francis's voice in her ear, when Mrs. Maxwell began pouring the tea.

"Real pleasant," said Lois.

Mrs. Maxwell had on her black gloves pouring the tea. The women eyed them surreptitiously. She wore them always in company, but this was an innovation. They did not know how she had put them on to conceal the burn in her wrist which she had gotten in her blind fury as she flew about the kitchen preparing supper, handling all the household utensils as if they were weapons to attack Providence.

Mrs. Maxwell poured the tea and portioned out the sugar with her black-gloved hands, and Mrs. Field stiffly buttered her biscuits. Nobody dreamed of the wolves at the vitals of these two old women.

However, the eyes of the guests from the first had wandered to a cake in the centre of the table. It was an oblong black cake; it was set on a plate surrounded thickly with sprigs of myrtle, and upon the top lay a little bouquet of white flowers and green leaves. Mrs. Lowe and Mrs. Robbins, who sat side by side, looked at each other. Mrs. Lowe's eyes said, "*Is* that a wedding-cake?" and Mrs. Robbin's said: "I dunno; it ain't frosted. It looks jest like a loaf she's had on hand."

But nothing could exceed the repose and dignity with which Mrs. Maxwell, at the last stage of the meal, requested her nephew to pass the cake to her. Nobody could have dreamed as she cut it, every turn of her burned wrist giving her pain, of the frantic haste with which she had taken that old fruit cake out of the jar down-cellar, and pulled those sprigs of myrtle from the bank under the north windows.

"Will you have some weddin'-cake?" said she.

The ladies each took a slice gingerly and respectfully. Mrs. Lowe and Mrs. Robbins nodded to each other imperceptibly. The cake was not iced with those fine devices which usually make a wedding-loaf, it was rather dry, and not particularly rich; but Mrs. Maxwell's perfect manner as she cut and served it, her acting on her own little histrionic stage, had swayed them to her will. Mrs. Lowe and Mrs. Robbins both thought she knew. But the minister's wife still doubted; and later, when the other women were removed from the spell of her acting, their old suspicions returned. It was always a mooted question in Elliot whether or not Mrs. Jane Maxwell had known of her daughter's marriage. Not all her subsequent behavior, her meeting the young couple with open arms at the station on their return, and Flora's appearance at church the next Sunday in the silk dress which her mother had concocted during her absence, could quite allay the suspicion, although it prevented it from gaining ground.

All that evening Mrs. Maxwell's courage never flagged. She entertained her guests as well as a woman of Sparta could have done. She even had the coolness to prosecute other projects which she had in mind. She kept Mrs. Field and Lois behind the rest, and walked home with the mother, that Francis might have the girl to himself. And she went into the house with Mrs. Field, and slipped a parcel into her pocket, while the two young people had a parting word at the gate.

CHAPTER VII

It was a hot afternoon in August. Amanda Pratt had set all her windows wide open, but no breeze came in, only the fervid breath of the fields and the white road outside.

She sat at a front window and darned a white stocking; her long, thin arms and her neck showed faintly through her old loose muslin sacque. The muslin was white, with a close-set lavender sprig, and she wore a cameo brooch at her throat. The blinds were closed, and she had to bend low over her mending in order to see in the green gloom.

Mrs. Babcock came toiling up the bank to the house, but Amanda did not notice her until she reached the front door. Then she fetched a great laboring sigh.

"Oh, hum!" said she, audibly, in a wrathful voice; "if I'd had any idea of it, I wouldn't have come a step."

Then Amanda looked out with a start. "Is that you, Mis' Babcock?" she called hospitably through the blind.

"Yes, it's me — what's left of me. Oh, hum! Oh, hum!"

Amanda ran and opened the door, and Mrs. Babcock entered, panting. She had a green umbrella, which she furled with difficulty at the door, and a palm-leaf fan. Her face, in the depths of her scooping green barége bonnet, was dank with perspiration, and scowling with indignant misery. She sank into a chair, and fanned herself with a desperate air.

Amanda set her umbrella in the corner, then she stood looking sympathetically at her. "It's a pretty hot day, ain't it?" said she.

"I should think 'twas hot. Oh, hum!"

"Don't you want me to get you a tumbler of water?"

"I dunno. I don't drink much cold water; it don't agree with me very well. Oh, dear! You ain't got any of your beer made, I s'pose?"

"Oh, no, I ain't. I'm dreadful sorry. Don't you want a swaller of cold tea?"

"Well, I dunno but I'll have jest a swaller, if you've got some. Oh, dear me, hum!"

Amanda went out hurriedly, and returned with a britannia teapot and a tumbler. She poured out some tea, and Mrs. Babcock drank with desperate gulps.

"I think cold tea is better for anybody than cold water in hot weather," said Amanda. "Won't you have another swaller, Mis' Babcock?"

Mrs. Babcock shook her head, and Amanda carried the teapot and tumbler back to the kitchen, then she seated herself again, and resumed her mending. Mrs. Babcock fanned and panted, and eyed Amanda.

"You look cool enough in that old muslin sacque," said she, in a tone of vicious injury.

"Yes, it is real cool. I've kept this sacque on purpose for a real hot day."

"Well, it's dreadful long in the shoulder seams, 'cordin' to the way they make 'em now, but I s'pose it's cool. Oh, hum! I ruther guess I shouldn't have come out of the house, if I'd any idea how hot 'twas in the sun. Seems to me it's hot as an oven here. I should think you'd air off your house early in the mornin', an' then shut your windows tight, an' keep the heat out."

"I know some folks do that way," said Amanda.

"Well, I always do, an' I guess 'most everybody does that's good housekeepers. It makes a sight of difference."

Amanda said nothing, but she sat straighter.

"I s'pose you don't have to make any fire from mornin' till night; seems as if you might keep cool."

"No, I don't have to."

"Well, I do. There I had to go to work to-day an' cook squash an' beans an' green corn. The men folks ain't satisfied if they don't have 'em in the time of 'em. I wish sometimes there wasn't no such thing as garden sauce. I tell 'em sometimes I guess if they had to get the things ready an' cook 'em themselves, they'd go without. Seems sometimes as if the whole creation was like a kitchen without any pump in it, specially contrived to make women folks extra work. Looks to me as if pease without pods could have been contrived pretty easy, and it does seem as if there wasn't any need of havin' strings on the beans."

"Mis' Green has got a kind of beans without any strings," said Amanda. "She brought me over some the other day, an' they were about the best I ever eat."

"Well, I know there is a kind without strings," returned Mrs. Babcock; "but I ain't got none in my garden, an' I never shall have. It ain't my lot to have things come easy. Seems as if it got hotter an' hotter. Why don't you open your front door?"

"Jest as sure as I do, the house will be swarmin' with flies."

"You'd ought to have a screen-door. I made Adoniram make me one five years ago, an' it's a real nice one; but I know, of course, you ain't got nobody to make one for you. Once in a while it seems as if men folks come in kinder handy, an' they'd ought to, when women work an' slave the way I do to fill 'em up. Mebbe some time when Adoniram ain't drove, I could get him to make a door for you. Mebbe some time next winter."

"I s'pose it would be nice," replied Amanda. "You're real kind to offer, Mis' Babcock."

"Well, I s'pose women that have men folks to do for 'em ought to be kind of obligin' sometimes to them that ain't. I'll see if I can get Adoniram to make you a screen-door next winter. Seems to me it does get hotter an' hotter. For the land sakes, Amanda Pratt! what are you cuttin' that great hole in that stockin' heel for? Are you crazy?"

Amanda colored. "The other stockin's got a hole in it," said she, "an' I'm makin' 'em match."

"Cuttin' a great big hole in a stockin' heel on purpose to darn? Mandy Pratt, you ain't?"

"I am," replied Amanda, with dignity.

"Well, if you ain't a double and twisted old maid!" gasped Mrs. Babcock.

Amanda's long face and her neck were a delicate red.

Mrs. Babcock laughed a loud, sarcastic cackle. "I never — did!" she giggled.

Amanda opened her mouth as if to speak, then she shut it tightly, remembering the offer of the screen-door. She had had so few gifts in her whole life that she had a meek impulse of gratitude even if one were thrust into her hand hard enough to hurt her.

"Well," Mrs. Babcock continued, still sniggering unpleasantly, "I don't want to hurt your feelin's, Mandy; you needn't color up so; but I can't help laughin'."

"Laugh, then, if you want to," said Amanda, with a quick flash. She forgot the screen-door.

Mrs. Babcock drew her face down quickly. "Land, Mandy," said she, "don't get mad. I didn't mean anything. Anybody knows that old maids is jest as good as them that gets married. I ain't told you what I come over here for. I declare I got so terrible heated up, I couldn't think of nothin'. Look here, Mandy."

Amanda mended on the stocking foot drawn tightly over her left hand, and did not raise her eyes.

"Mandy, you ain't mad, be you? You know I didn't mean nothin'."

"I ain't mad," replied Amanda, in a constrained tone.

"Well, there ain't nothin' to be mad about. Look here, Mandy, how long is it since Mis' Field and Lois went?"

"About three months."

"Look here! I dunno what you'll say, but I think Mis' Green thought real favorable of it. Do you know how cheap you can go down to Boston an' back now?"

Amanda looked up. "No. Why?" said she.

Mrs. Babcock stopped fanning and leaned forward. "Amanda Pratt, you can go down to Boston an' back, an' be gone a week, for — three dollars an' sixty cents."

Amanda stared back at her in a startled way.

"Let's you an' me an' Mis' Green go down an' see Mis' Field an' Lois," said Mrs. Babcock, in a tragic voice.

Amanda turned pale. "They don't live in Boston," she said, with a bewildered air.

"We can go down to Boston on the early train," replied Mrs. Babcock, importantly. "Then we can have all the afternoon to go round Boston an' see the sights, an' then, toward night, we can go out to Mis' Field's. Land, here's Mis' Green now! She said she'd come over as soon as Abby got home from school. I'm jest tellin' her about it, Mis' Green."

Mrs. Green stood in the doorway, smiling half-shamefacedly. "I s'pose you think it's a dreadful silly plan, Mandy," said she deprecatingly.

Amanda got up and pushed the rocking-chair in which she had been sitting toward the new-comer.

"Set down, do," said she. "I dunno, Mis' Green. I ain't had time to think it over, it's come so sudden." Amanda's face was collected, but her voice was full of agitation.

"Well," said Mrs. Green, "I ain't known which end my head is on since Mis' Babcock come in an' spoke of it. First I thought I couldn't go nohow, an' I dunno as I can now. Still, it does seem dreadful cheap to go down to Boston an' back, an' I ain't been down more'n four times in the last twenty years. I ain't been out gaddin' much, an' that's a fact."

"The longer you set down in one corner, the longer you can," remarked Mrs. Babcock. "I believe in goin' while you've got a chance, for my part."

"I ain't ever been to Boston," said Amanda, and her face had the wishful, far-away look that her grandfather's might have had when he thought of the sea.

"It does seem as if you'd ought to go once," said Mrs. Green.

"I say, let's start up an' go!" cried Mrs. Babcock, in an intense voice.

The three women looked at each other.

"Abby could keep house for father a few days," said Mrs.

Green, as if to some carping judge; "an' it ain't goin' to cost much, an' I know father'd say go."

"Well, I guess I can cook up enough victuals to last Adoniram and the boys whilst I'm gone," said Mrs. Babcock defiantly; "I guess they can get along. Adoniram can make rye puddin', an' they can fill up on rye puddin' an' molasses. I'm a-goin'."

"I dunno," said Amanda, trembling. "I'm dreadful afraid I hadn't ought to."

"Well, I should think you could go, if Mis' Green an' I could," said Mrs. Babcock. "Here you ain't got nobody but jest yourself, an' ain't got to leave a thing cooked up nor nothin'."

"I would like to see Mis' Field an' Lois again, but it seems like a great undertakin'," sighed Amanda. "Then it's goin' to cost something."

"It ain't goin' to cost but jest three dollars an' sixty cents," said Mrs. Babcock. "I guess you can afford that, Mandy. There your tenement didn't stay vacant two weeks after the Fields went; the Simmonses came right in. I guess if I had rent-money, an' nobody but myself, I could afford to travel once in a while."

"Now you'd better make up your mind to go, Mandy," Mrs. Green said. "I think Mis' Field would be more pleased to see you than anybody in Green River. That's one thing I think about goin'. I know she'll be tickled almost to death to see us comin' in. Mis' Field's a real good woman. There wa'n't anybody in town I set more by than I did by her."

"When did you hear from her last, Mandy?" interposed Mrs. Babcock.

"About a month ago."

"I s'pose Lois is a good deal better?"

"Yes, I guess she is. Her mother said she seemed pretty well for her. I s'pose it agrees with her better down there."

"I s'pose there was a good deal more fuss made about her when she was here than there was any need of," said Mrs. Babcock, her whole face wrinkled upward contemptuously; "a great deal more fuss. There wa'n't nothin' ailed the girl if folks had let her alone, talkin' an' scarin' her mother to death. She was jest kind of run down with the spring weather. Young girls wilt down dreadful easy, an' spring up again. I've seen 'em. 'Twa'n't nothin'."

"Well, I dunno; she looked dreadfully," Mrs. Green said, with mild opposition.

"Well, you can see how much it amounted to," returned Mrs. Babcock, with a triumphant sniff. "Folks ought to have been ashamed of themselves, scarin' Mis' Field the way they did about her. Seemed as if they was determined to have Lois go into consumption whether or no, an' was goin' to push her in, if they couldn't manage it in no other way. I s'pose you've sent all Mis' Field's things down there, Mandy?"

"The furniture is all up garret," said Amanda. "All I've sent down was their clothes. Mis' Field had me pack 'em up in their two trunks, an' send 'em down to Lois. I didn't see why she didn't have me mark 'em to her."

"I should think it was kind of queer," said Mrs. Green. "Now s'pose we go, what had we better carry for clothes? We don't need no trunk."

"Of course we don't," said Mrs. Babcock promptly. "We can each carry a bag. We ain't going to need much."

"I guess, if I went," said Amanda, "that I should carry this sacque to slip on, if it's as hot weather as 'tis now. I should have to do it up, but that ain't much work."

Mrs. Babcock eyed it. "Well, I dunno," said she; "it's pretty long in the shoulders seams. I dunno how much they dress down there where Mis' Field lives. Mebbe 'twould do."

"There's one thing I've been thinkin' about," Mrs. Green said, with an anxious air. "If we go down on that early train, an' stay all day in Boston, we shall have to buy us something to eat; we should get dreadful faint before we got out to Mis' Field's, and things are dreadful high in those places."

"Oh, land!" cried Mrs. Babcock in a superior tone. "All we've got to do is to carry some luncheon with us. I'll make some pies, and you can bake some cookies, an' then we'll set down in Boston Common an' eat it. That's the way lots of folks do. That ain't nothin' to worry about. Well, now, I think it's about time for us to decide whether or no we're goin'. I've got to go home an' git supper."

"I'll do jest as the rest say," said Mrs. Green. "I s'pose I can go. I s'pose father'll say I'd better. An' Abby she was all for it, when I spoke about it to her. She thinks she can have the Fay girl over to stay with her, an' she wants me to buy her a dress in Boston, instead of gettin' it here."

"Well," said Amanda, with a sigh — she was quite pale — "I'll think of it."

"We've got to make up our minds," said Mrs. Babcock sharply. "There ain't time for much thinkin'. The excursion starts a day after to-morrow."

"I'll have my mind made up to-morrow mornin'," said Amanda. "I've got to think of it over-night, anyhow. I can't start right up an' say I'll go, without a minute to think about it." Her voice trembled nervously, but decision underlay it.

"I don't see why it ain't time enough if we decide to-morrow morning. I'd ruther like to think of it a little while longer," said Mrs. Green.

Mrs. Babcock got up. "Well," said she, "I'll send Adoniram round to-morrow mornin', an' you tell him what you've decided. I guess I shall go whether or no. I've got three men folks to leave, an' it's a good deal more of an undertakin' for me than some, but I ain't easy scart. I b'lieve in goin' once in a while."

"Well, I'll let you know in the mornin'. I jest want to think of it over-night," repeated Amanda, with dignified apology.

She went to the door with her guests. Mrs. Babcock spread her green umbrella, and descended the steps with a stiff side-wise motion.

"It is hotter than ever, I do believe," she groaned.

"Well, now, I was jest thinkin' it was a little grain cooler," returned Mrs. Green, following in her wake. Her back was meekly bent; her face, shaded by a black sun-hat, was thrust forward with patient persistency. "There, I feel a little breeze now," she added.

"I guess all the breeze there is, is in your own motion," retorted Mrs. Babcock. Her green umbrella bobbed energetically. She fanned at every step.

"Mebbe it's your fan," said the other woman.

Amanda went into the house and shut the door. She stood in the middle of the parlor and looked around. There was a certain amaze in her eyes, as if everything wore a new aspect. "They can talk all they've a mind to," she muttered, "it's a great undertakin'. S'pose anything happened? If anything happened to them whilst they were gone, there's folks enough to home to see to things. S'pose anything happened to me, there ain't anybody. If I go, I've got to leave this house jest so. I've got to be sure the bureau drawers are all packed up, an' things swept an' dusted, so folks won't make remarks. There's other things, too. Everything's got to be thought of. There's the cat. I s'pose I could get Abby Green to come over an' feed her, but I dassen't trust her. Young girls ain't to be depended on. Ten chances to one she'd get to carryin' on with that Fay girl an' forgit all about that cat. She won't lap her milk out of anything but a clean saucer, neither, and I don't believe Abby would look out for that. She always seemed to me kind of heedless. I dunno about the whole of it."

Amanda shook her head; her eyes were dilated; there was an anxious and eager expression in her face. She went into the kitchen, kindled the fire, and made herself a cup of tea, which she drank absently. She could not eat anything.

The cat came mewing at the door, and she let her in and fed her. "I dunno how she'd manage," she said, as she watched her lap the milk from the clean saucer beside the cooking-stove.

After she had put away the cat's saucer and her own tea-cup, she stood hesitating.

"Well, I don't care," said she, in a decisive tone; "I'm goin' to do it. It's got to be done, anyhow, whether I go or not. It's been on my mind for some time."

Amanda got out her best black dress from the closet, and sat down to alter the shoulder seams. "I don't care nothin' about this muslin sacque," said she, "but I ain't goin' to have Mis' Babcock measurin' my shoulder seams every single minute if I do go, an' they may be real dressy down where Mis' Field is."

Amanda sewed until ten o'clock; then she went to bed, but she slept little. She was up early the next morning. Adoniram Babcock came over about eight o'clock; the windows and blinds were all flung wide open, the braided rugs lay out in the yard. He put his gentle grizzled face in at one of the windows. There was a dusty odor. Amanda was sweeping vigorously, with a white handkerchief tied over her head. Her delicate face was all of a deep pink color.

"Ann Lizy sent over to see if you'd made up your mind," said Adoniram.

Amanda started. "Good-mornin', Mr. Babcock. Yes, you can tell her I have. I'm a-goin'."

There was a reckless defiance of faith in Amanda's voice. She had a wild air as she stood there with the broom in a faint swirl of dust.

"Well, Ann Lizy'll be glad you've made up your mind to. She's gone to bakin'," said the old man in the window.

"I've got to bake some, too," said Amanda. She began sweeping again.

"I've jest been over to Mis' Green's, an' she says she's goin' if you do," said Mr. Babcock.

"Well, you tell her I'm goin'," said Amanda, with a long breath.

"I guess you'll have a good time," said the old man, turning away. "I tell Ann Lizy she can stay a month if she wants to. Me an' the boys can git along." He laughed a pleasant chuckle as he went off.

Amanda glanced after him. "I shouldn't care if I had a man to leave to look after the house," said she.

Amanda toiled all day; she swept and dusted every room in her little domicile. She put all her bureau drawers and closets in exquisite order. She did not neglect even the cellar and the garret. Mrs. Babcock, looking in at night, found her rolling out sugar gingerbread.

"For the land sakes, Mandy!" said she, "what are you cookin' by lamp-light for this awful hot night?"

"I'm makin' a little short gingerbread for luncheon."

"I don't see what you left it till this time of day for. What you got them irons on the stove for?"

"I've got to iron my muslin sacque. I've got it all washed and starched."

"Ironin' this time of day! I'd like to know what you've been doin' ever since you got up?"

"I've been getting everything in order, in case anything happened," replied Amanda. She tried to speak with cool composure, but her voice trembled. Her dignity failed her in this unwonted excitement.

"What's goin' to happen, for the land sake?" cried Mrs. Babcock.

"I dunno. None of us know. Things do happen sometimes."

Mrs. Babcock stared at her, half in contempt, half in alarm. "I hope you ain't had no forewarnin' that you ain't goin' to live nor anything," said she. "If you have, I should think you'd better stay to home."

"I ain't had no more forewarnin' than anybody," said Amanda. "All is, there ain't nobody in the other part of the house. The Simmonses all went yesterday to make a visit at her mother's, and in case anything should happen, I'm goin' to leave things lookin' so I'm willin' anybody should see 'em."

"Well," said Mrs. Babcock, "I guess you couldn't leave things so you'd be willin' anybody'd see 'em if you had three men folks afoul of 'em for three days. I've got to be goin' if I git up for that four-o'clock train in the mornin'. I've made fifteen pies an' five loaves of bread, besides bakin' beans, to say nothin' of a great panful of doughnuts an' some cake. I ain't been up garret nor down cellar cleanin', an' if anything happens to me, I s'pose folks'll see some dust and cobwebs, but I've done considerable. Adoniram's goin' to take us all down in the covered wagon; he'll be round about half-past four."

Amanda lighted Mrs. Babcock out the front door; then she returned to her tasks. She did not go to bed that night. She had put her bedroom in perfect order, and would not disturb it. She lay down on her hard parlor sofa awhile, but she slept very little. At two o'clock she kindled a fire, made some tea, and cooked an egg for her breakfast. Then she arrayed herself in her best dress. She was all ready, her bag and basket of luncheon packed and her bonnet on, at three o'clock. She sat down and folded her hands to wait, but presently started up. "I'm going to do it," said she. "I don't care, I am. I can't feel easy unless I do."

She got some writing-paper and pen and ink from the chimney cupboard and sat down at the table. She wrote rapidly, her lips pursed, her head to one side. Then she folded the paper, wrote on the outside, and arranged it conspicuously on the top of a leather-covered Bible on the centre of the table. "There!" said she. "It ain't regular, I s'pose, an' I ain't had any lawyer, but I guess they'd carry out my wishes if anything happened to me. I ain't got nobody but Cousin Rhoda Hill, an' Cousin Maria Bennet; an' Rhoda don't need a cent, an' Maria'd ought to have it all. This house will make her real comfortable, an' my clothes will fit her. I s'pose I'd have this dress on, but my black alpaca's pretty good. I s'pose Mis' Babcock would laugh, but I feel a good deal easier about goin'."

Amanda waited again; she blew out her lamp, for the early dawnlight strengthened. She listened intently for wheels, and looked anxiously at the clock. "It would be dreadful if we got left, after all," she said.

Suddenly the covered wagon came in sight; the white horse trotted at a good pace. Adoniram held the reins and his wife sat beside him. Mrs. Green peered out from the back seat. "Mandy! Mandy!" Mrs. Babcock called, before they reached the gate. But Amanda was already on the front door-step, fitting the key in the lock.

"I'm all ready," she answered, "jest as soon as I can get the door locked."

"We ain't got any too much time," cried Mrs. Babcock.

Amanda went down the path with her basket and black valise and parasol. Adoniram got out and helped her into the wagon. She had to climb over the front seat. As they drove off she leaned out and gazed back at the house. Her tortoise-shell cat was coming around the corner. "I do hope the cat will get along all right," she said agitatedly. "I've fed her this mornin', an' I've left her enough milk till I get back — a saucerful for each day — an' Abby said she'd give her all the scraps off the table, you know, Mis' Green."

Mrs. Babcock turned around. "Now, Amanda Pratt," said she,

"I'd like to know how in creation you've left a saucerful of milk for that cat for every day till you get back."

"I set ten saucers full of milk down cellar," replied Amanda, still staring back anxiously at the cat — "one for each day. I got extra milk last night on purpose. She likes it jest as well if it's sour, if the saucer's clean."

Amanda looked up with serious wonder at Mrs. Babcock, who was laughing shrilly. Mrs. Green, too, was smiling, and Adoniram chuckled.

"For the land sakes, Amanda Pratt!" gasped Mrs. Babcock, "you don't s'pose that cat is goin' to stint herself to a saucer a day? Why, she'll eat half of it all up before night."

Amanda stood up in the carriage. "I've got to go back, that's all," said she. "I ain't goin' to have that cat starve."

"Land sakes, set down!" cried Mrs. Babcock. "She won't starve. She can hunt."

"Abby'll feed her, I know," said Mrs. Green, pulling gently at her companion's arm. "Don't you worry, Mandy."

"Well, I guess I shouldn't worry about a cat with claws to catch mice in warm weather," said Mrs. Babcock, with a sarcastic titter. "It's goin' to be a dreadful hot day. Set down, Mandy. There ain't no use talkin' about goin' back. There ain't any time. Mis' Green an' me ain't goin' to stay to home on account of a cat."

Amanda subsided weakly. She felt strange, and not like herself. Mrs. Babcock seemed to recognize it by some subtle intuition. She would never have dared use such a tone toward her without subsequent concessions. Amanda had always had a certain dignity and persistency which had served to intimidate too presuming people; now she had lost it all.

"I'll write to Abby, jest as soon as I get down there, to give the cat her milk," whispered Mrs. Green soothingly; and Amanda was comforted.

The covered wagon rolled along the country road toward the railroad station. Adoniram drove, and the three women sat up straight, and looked out with a strange interest, as if they had never seen the landscape before. The meadows were all filmy with cobwebs; there were patches of corn in the midst of them, and the long blades drooped limply. The flies swarmed thickly over the horse's back. The air was scalding; there was a slight current of cool freshness from the dewy ground, but it would soon be gone.

"It ain't goin' to rain," said Mrs. Babcock, "there's cobwebs on the grass, but it's goin' to be terrible hot."

They reached the station fifteen minutes before the train.

After Adoniram had driven away, they sat in a row on a bench on the platform, with their baggage around them. They did not talk much; even Mrs. Babcock looked serious and contemplative in this momentary lull. Their thoughts reached past and beyond them to the homes they had left, and the new scenes ahead.

When the whistle of the train sounded they all stood up, and grasped their valises tightly. Mrs. Green looked toward the coming train; her worn face under her black bonnet, between its smooth curves of gray hair, had all the sensitive earnestness which comes from generations of high breeding. She was, on her father's side, of a race of old New England ministers.

"Well, I dunno but I've been pretty faithful, an' minded my household the way women are enjoined to in the Scriptures; mebbe it's right for me to take this little vacation," she said, and her serious eyes were full of tears.

CHAPTER VIII

When Jane Field, in her assumed character, had lived three months in Elliot, she was still unsuspected. She was not liked, and that made her secret safer. She was full of dogged resolution and audacity. She never refused to see a caller nor accept an invitation, but people never called upon her nor invited her when they could avoid it, and thus she was not so often exposed to contradictions and inconsistencies which might have betrayed her. Elliot people not only disliked her, they were full of out-spoken indignation against her. The defiant, watchful austerity which made her repel when she intended to encourage their advances had turned them against her, but more than that her supposed ill-treatment of her orphan niece.

When Lois, the third week of her stay in Elliot, had gone to a dressmaker and asked for some sewing to do, the news was well over the village by night. "That woman, who has all John Maxwell's money, is too stingy and mean to support her niece, and she too delicate to work," people said. The dressmaker to whom Lois appealed did not for a minute hesitate to give her work, although she had already many women sewing for her, and she had just given some to Mrs. Maxwell's daughter Flora.

"There!" said she, when Lois had gone out. "I ain't worth five hundred dollars in the world, I don't know how she'll sew, and I didn't need any extra help — it's takin' it right out of my pocket, likely as not — but I couldn't turn off a cat that looked up at me the way that child did. She looks pinched. I don't believe that old woman gives her enough to eat. Of all the mean work — worth all that money, and sending her niece out to get sewing to do! I don't believe but what she's most starved her."

It was true that Lois for the last week had not had enough to eat, but neither had her mother. The two had been eking out the remnants of Lois's school-money as best they might. There were many provisions in the pantry and cellar of the Maxwell house, but they would touch none of them. Some money which Mr. Tuxbury had paid to Mrs. Field — the first instalment from the revenue of her estate — she had put carefully away in a sugar-bowl on the top shelf of the china closet, and had not spent a penny of it. After Lois began to sew, her slender earnings provided them with the most frugal fare. Mrs. Field eked it out in every way that she could. She had a little vegetable garden and kept a few hens. As the season advanced, she scoured the berry pastures, and spent many hours stooping painfully over the low bushes. Three months from the time at which she came to Elliot, on the day on which her neighbors started from Green River to visit her, she was out in the pasture trying to fill her pail with blueberries. All the sunlight seemed to centre on her black figure like a burning-glass; the thick growth of sweet-fern around the blueberry bushes sent a hot and stifling aroma into her face; the wild flowers hung limply, like delicate painted rags, and the rocks were like furnaces. Mrs. Field went out soon after dinner, and at half-past five she was still picking; the berries were not very plentiful.

Lois, at home, wondered why she did not return, and the more because there was a thunder-storm coming up. There was a heavy cloud in the northwest, and a steady low rumble of thunder. Lois sat out in the front yard sewing; her face was pink and moist with the heat; the sleeves of her old white muslin dress clung to her arms. Presently the gate clicked, and Mrs. Jane Maxwell's daughter Flora came toward her over the grass.

"Hullo!" said she.

"Hullo!" returned Lois.

"It's a terrible day — isn't it?"

"Terrible!"

Lois got up, but Flora would not take her chair. She sat down clumsily on the pine needles, and fanned herself with the cover of a book she carried.

"I've just been down to the library, an' got this book," she remarked.

"Is it good?"

"They say it's real good. Addie Green's been reading it."

Flora wore a bright blue cambric dress and a brown straw hat. Her figure was stout and high-shouldered, her dull-complexioned face full of placid force. She was not very young, and she looked much older than she was; and people had wondered how George Freeman, who was handsome and much courted by the girls, as well as younger than she, had come to marry her. They also wondered how her mother, who had been so bitterly opposed to the match, had given in, and was now living so amicably with the young couple; they had been on the alert for a furious village feud. But when Flora and her husband had returned from their stolen wedding tour, Mrs. Maxwell had met them at the depot and bidden them home with her with vociferous ardor, and the next Sunday Flora had gone to church in the new silk. There had been a conflict of two wills, and one had covered its defeat with a parade of victory. Mrs. Maxwell had talked a great deal about her daughter's marriage and how well she had done.

"There's a thunder-shower coming up," Flora said after a little. "Where's your aunt?"

"Gone berrying."

"She'll get caught in the shower if she don't look out. What makes you work so steady this hot day, Lois?"

"I've got to get this done."

"There isn't any need of your working so hard."

Lois said nothing.

"If your aunt ain't willing to do for you it's time you had somebody else to," persisted Flora. "I wish I had had the money on your account. I wouldn't have let you work so. You look better than you did when you came here, but you look tired. I heard somebody else say so the other day."

Flora said the last with a meaning smile.

Lois blushed.

"Yes, I did," Flora repeated. "I don't suppose you can guess who 'twas?"

Lois said nothing; she bent her hot face closer over her work.

"See here, Lois," said Flora. She hesitated with her eyes fixed warily on Lois; then she went on: "What makes you treat Francis so queer lately?"

"I didn't know I had," replied Lois, evasively.

"You don't treat him a bit the way you did at first."

"I don't know what you mean, Flora."

"Well, if you don't, it's no matter," returned Flora. "Francis hasn't said anything about it to me; you needn't think he has. All is, you'll never find a better fellow than he is, Lois Field, I don't care where you go."

Flora spoke with slow warmth. Lois's face quivered. "If you don't take care you'll never get married at all," said Flora, half laughing.

Lois sat up straight. "I shall never get married to anybody," said she. "That's one thing I won't do. I'll die first."

Flora stared at her. "Why, why not?" said she.

"I won't."

"I never knew what happiness was until I got married," said Flora. Then she flushed up suddenly all over her steady face.

Lois, too, started and blushed, as if the other girl's speech had struck some answering chord in her. The two were silent a moment. Lois sewed; Flora stared off through the trees at the darkening sky. The low rumble of thunder was incessant.

"George is one of the best husbands that ever a girl had," said Flora, in a tender, shamed voice; "but Francis would make just as good a one."

Lois made no reply. She almost turned her back toward Flora as she sewed.

"I guess you'll change your mind some time about getting married," Flora said.

"No, I never will," returned Lois.

"Well, I suppose if you don't, you'll have money enough to take care of yourself with some time, as far as that goes," said Flora. Her voice had a sarcastic ring.

"I shall never have one cent of that Maxwell money," said Lois, with sudden fire. "I'll tell you that much, once for all!" Her eyes fairly gleamed in her delicate, burning face.

"Why, you scare me! What is the matter?" cried Flora.

Lois took a stitch. "Nothing," said she.

"You'd ought to have the money, of course," said Flora, in a bewildered way. "Who else would have it?"

"I don't know," said Lois. "You are the one that ought to have it."

Flora laughed. "Land, I don't want it!" said she. "George earns plenty for us to live on. She's your own aunt, and of course she'll have to leave it to you, if she does act so miserly with it now. There, I know she's your aunt, Lois, and I don't suppose I ought to speak so, but I can't help it. After all, it don't make much difference, or it needn't, whether you have it or not. I've begun to think money is the very least part of anything in this world, and I want you to be looking out for something else, too, Lois."

"I can't look out for money, or something else, either. You don't know," said Lois, in a pitiful voice.

There came a flash, and then a great crash of thunder. The tempest was about to break.

Flora started up abruptly. "I must run," she shouted through a sudden gust of wind. "Good-by."

Flora sped out of the yard. Her blue dress, lashing around her feet, changed color in the ghastly light of the storm. Some flying leaves struck her in the face. At the gate a cloud of dust from the road nearly blinded her. She realized in a bewildered fashion that there were three women on the other side struggling frantically with the latch.

"Does Mis' Jane Field live here?" inquired one of them, breathlessly.

"No," replied Flora; "that isn't her name."

"She don't?"

"No," gasped Flora, her head lowered before the wind.

"Well, I want to know, ain't this the old Maxwell place?"

"Yes," said Flora.

Some great drops of rain began to fall; there was another flash. The woman struggled mightily, and prevailed over the gate-latch. She pushed it open. "Well, I don't care," said she, "I'm comin' in, whether or no. I dunno but my bonnet-strings will spot, an' I ain't goin' to have my best clothes soaked. It's mighty funny nobody knows where Mis' Field lives; but this is the old Maxwell house, where she wrote Mandy she lived, an' I'm goin' in."

Flora stood aside, and the three women entered with a rush. Lois, standing near the door front, saw them coming through the greenish-yellow gloom, their three black figures scudding before the wind like black-sailed ships.

"Land sakes!" shrieked out Mrs. Babcock, "there's Lois now! Lois, how are you? I'd like to know what that girl we met at the gate meant telling us they didn't live here. Why, Lois Field, how do you do? Where's your mother? I guess we'd better step right in, an' not stop to talk. It's an awful tempest. I'm dreadful afraid my bonnet trimmin' will spot."

They all scurried up the steps and into the house. Then the women turned and kissed Lois, and raised a little clamor of delight over her. She stood panting. She did not ask them into the sitting-room. Her head whirled. It seemed to her that the end of everything had come.

But Mrs. Babcock turned toward the sitting-room door. She had pulled off her bonnet, and was wiping it anxiously with her handkerchief. "This is the way, ain't it?" she said.

Lois followed them in helplessly. The room was dark as night, for the shutters were closed. Mrs. Babcock flung one open peremptorily.

"We'll break our necks here, if we don't have some light," she said. The hail began to rattle on the window-panes.

"It's hailin'!" the women chorussed.

"Are your windows all shut?" Mrs. Babcock demanded of Lois.

And the girl said, in a dazed way, that the bedroom windows were open, and then went mechanically to shut them.

"Shut the blinds, too!" screamed Mrs. Babcock. "The hail's comin' in this side terrible heavy. I'm afraid it'll break the glass." Mrs. Babcock herself, her face screwed tightly against an onslaught of wind and hail, shut the blinds, and the room was again plunged in darkness. "We'll have to stan' it," said she. "Mis' Field don't want her windows all broke in. That's dreadful sharp."

Thunder shook the house like an explosion. The women looked at each other with awed faces.

"Where is your mother? Why don't she come in here?" Mrs. Babcock asked excitedly of Lois returning from the bedroom.

"She's gone berrying," replied Lois, feebly. She sank into a chair.

"Gone berryin'!" screamed Mrs. Babcock, and the other women echoed her.

"Yes'm."

"When did she go?"

"Right after dinner."

"Right after dinner, an' she ain't got home yet! Out in this awful tempest! Well, she'll be killed. You'll never see her again, that's all. A berry pasture is the most dangerous place in creation in a thunder-shower. Out berryin' in all this hail an' thunder an' lightnin'!"

Mrs. Green pressed close up to Lois. "Ain't you any idea where she's gone?" said she. "If you have, I'll jest slip off my dress skirt, an' you give me an old shawl, an' I'll go with you an' see if we can't find her."

"I'll go, too," cried Amanda. "Don't you know which way they went, Lois?"

Just then the south side-door slammed sharply.

"She's come," said Lois, in a strained voice.

"Well, I'm thankful!" cried Mrs. Green. "Hadn't you better run out an' help her off with her wet things, Lois?"

But the sitting-room door opened, and Mrs. Field stood there, a tall black shadow hardly shaped out from the gloom. The women all arose and hurried toward her. There was a shrill flurry of greeting. Mrs. Field's voice arose high and terrified above it.

"Who is it?" she cried out. "Who's here?"

"Why, your old neighbors, Mrs. Field. Don't you know us — Mandy an' Mis' Green an' Mis' Babcock? We come down on an excursion ticket to Boston — only three dollars an' sixty cents — an' we thought we'd surprise you."

"Ain't you dreadful wet, Mis' Field?" interposed Mrs. Green's solicitous voice.

"You'd better go and change your dress," said Amanda.

"When did you come?" said Mrs. Field.

"Jest now. For the land sakes, Mis' Field, your dress is soppin' wet! Do go an' change it, or you'll catch your death of cold."

Mrs. Field did not stir. The hail pelted on the windows. "Now, you go right along an' change it," cried Mrs. Babcock.

"Well," said Mrs. Field vaguely, "mebbe I'd better." She fumbled her way unsteadily toward her bedroom door.

"You go help her; it's dark as a pocket," said Mrs. Babcock imperatively to Lois; and the girl followed her mother.

"They act dreadful queer, seems to me," whispered Mrs. Babcock, when the bedroom door was closed.

"I guess it's jest because they're so surprised to see us," Mrs. Green whispered back.

"Well, if I ain't wanted, I can go back to where I come from, if I do have to throw the money away," Mrs. Babcock said, almost aloud. "I think they act queer, both on 'em. I should think they might seem a little mite more pleased to see three old neighbors so."

"Mebbe it's the thunder-shower that's kind of dazed 'em," said Amanda. She herself was much afraid of a thunder-shower. She had her feet well drawn up, and her hand over her eyes.

"It's a mercy Mis' Field wa'n't killed out in it," said Mrs. Green.

"I don't see what in creation she stayed out so in it for," rejoined Mrs. Babcock. "She must have seen the cloud comin' up. This is a pretty big house, ain't it? An' I should think it was furnished nice, near's I can see, but it's terrible old-fashioned."

Amanda huddled up in her chair, looked warily at the strange shadows in this unfamiliar room, and wished she were at home.

The storm increased rather than diminished. When Mrs. Field and Lois returned, all the women, at Mrs. Babcock's order, drew their chairs close together in the middle of the room.

"I've always heard that was the safest place," said she. "That was the way old Dr. Barnes always used to do. He had thirteen children; nine of 'em was girls. Whenever he saw a thunder-shower comin' up, he used to make Mis' Barnes an' the children go into the parlor, an' then they'd all set in the middle of the floor, an' he'd offer prayer. He used to say he'd do his part an' get in the safest place he knew of, an' then ask the Lord to help him. Mandy Pratt!"

"What say, Mis' Babcock?" returned Amanda, trembling.

"Have you got your hoop-skirt on?"

Amanda sprang up. "Yes, I have. I forgot it!"

"For the land sakes! I should think you'd thought of that, scared as you pretend to be in a thunder-shower. Do go in the bedroom an' drop it off this minute! Lois, you go with her."

While Amanda and Lois were gone there was a slight lull in the storm.

"I guess it's kind of lettin' up," said Mrs. Babcock. "This is a nice house you've got here, ain't it, Mis' Field?"

"Yes, 'tis," replied Jane Field.

"I s'pose there was a good deal of nice furniture in it, wa'n't there?"

"Considerable."

"Was there nice beddin'?"

"Yes."

"I s'pose there was plenty of table-cloths an' such things? Have you bought any new furniture, Mis' Field?"

"No, I ain't," said Mrs. Field. She moved her chair a little to make room for Lois and Amanda when they returned. Lois sat next her mother.

"I didn't know but you had. I thought mebbe the furniture was kind of old-fashioned. Have you — oh, ain't it awful?"

The storm had gathered itself like an animal for a fiercer onset. The room was lit up with a wild play of blue fire. The thunder crashed closely in its wake.

"Oh, we hadn't ought to talk of anything but the mercy of the Lord an' our sins!" wailed Mrs. Babcock. "Don't let's talk of anything else. That struck somewheres near. There's no knowin' where it'll come next. I never see such a shower. We don't have any like it in Green River. Oh, I hope we're all prepared!"

"That's the principal thing," said Mrs. Green, in a solemn trembling voice.

Amanda said nothing. She thought of her will; a vision of the nicely ordered rooms she had left seemed to show out before her in the flare of the lightning; in spite of her terror it was a comfort to her.

"We'd ought to be thankful in a time like this that we ain't any of us got any great wickedness on our consciences," said Mrs. Babcock. "It must be terrible for them that have, thinkin' they may die any minute when the next flash comes. I don't envy 'em."

"It must be terrible," assented Mrs. Green, like an amen.

"It's bad enough with the sins we've got on all our minds, the best of us," continued Mrs. Babcock. "Think how them that's broken God's commandments an' committed murders an' robberies must feel. I shouldn't think they could stan' it, unless they burst right out an' confessed to everybody — should you, Mis' Field?"

"I guess so," said Mrs. Field, in a hard voice.

Mrs. Babcock said no more; somehow she and the others felt repelled. They all sat in silence except for awed ejaculations when now and then came a louder crash of thunder. All at once, after a sharp flash, there was a wild clamor in the street; a bell clanged out.

"It's struck! it's struck!" shrieked Mrs. Babcock.

"Oh, it ain't this house, is it?" Amanda wailed.

They all rushed to the windows and flung open the blinds; a red glare filled the room; a large barn nearly opposite was on fire. They clutched each other, and watched the red gush of flame. The barn burned as if lighted at every corner.

"Are there any cows or horses in it?" panted Mrs. Babcock. "Oh, ain't it dreadful? Are there any, Mis' Field?"

"I dunno," said Mrs. Field.

She stood like a grim statue, the red light of the fire in her face. Lois was sobbing. Mrs. Green had put an arm around her.

"Don't, Lois, don't," she kept saying, in a solemn, agitated voice. "The Lord will overrule it all; it is He speakin' in it."

The women watched while the street filled with people, and the barn burned down. It did not take long. The storm began to lull rapidly. The thunder came at long intervals, and the hail turned into a gentle rain. Finally Mrs. Field went out into the kitchen to prepare supper, and Lois followed her.

"I never see anything like the way she acts," said Mrs. Babcock cautiously.

"She always was kind of quiet," rejoined Mrs. Green.

"Quiet! She acts as if she'd had thunder an' lightnin' an' hail an' barns burnt down every day since she's been here. I never see anybody act so queer."

"I 'most wish I'd stayed to home," said Amanda.

"Well, I wouldn't be backin' out the minute I'd got here, if I was you," returned Mrs. Babcock sharply. "It's comin' cooler, that's one thing, an' you won't need that white sacque. I should think you'd feel kinder glad of it, for them shoulder seams did look pretty long to what they wear 'em. An' I dare say folks here are pretty dressy. I declare I shall be kinder glad when supper's ready. I feel real faint to my stomach, as if I'd like somethin' hearty. I should have gone into one of them places in Boston if things hadn't been so awful dear."

But when Mrs. Field finally called them out to partake of the meal which she had prepared, there was little to satisfy an eager appetite. Nothing but the berries for which she had toiled so hard, a few thin slices of bread, no butter, and no tea, so little sugar in the bowl that the guests sprinkled it sparingly on their berries.

"I'll tell you what 'tis," Mrs. Babcock whispered when they

were upstairs in their chambers that night, "Mis' Field has grown tight since she got all that money. Sometimes it does work that way. I believe we should starve to death if we stayed here long. If it wa'n't for gittin' my money's worth, I should be for goin' home to-morrow. No butter an' no tea after we've come that long journey. I never heard of such a thing."

"I don't care anything about the butter and the tea," rejoined Amanda, "but I 'most feel as if I'd better go home to-morrow."

"If," said Mrs. Babcock, "you want to go home instead of gittin' the good of that excursion ticket, that you can stay a week on, you can, Amanda Pratt. I'm goin' to stay now, if it kills me."

CHAPTER IX

The three women from Green River had been six days in Elliot, they were going to leave the next morning, and Mrs. Field's secret had not been discovered. Nothing but her ill favor in the village had saved her. Nobody except Mrs. Jane Maxwell had come to call. Mrs. Babcock talked and wondered about it a great deal to Mrs. Green and Amanda.

"It's mighty queer, seems to me, that there ain't a soul but that one old woman set foot inside this house since we've been here," said she. "It don't look to me as if folks here thought much of Mis' Field. I know one thing: there couldn't three strange ladies come visitin' to Green River without I should feel as if I'd ought to go an' call an' find out who they was, an' pay 'em a little attention, if I thought anything at all of the folks they was visitin'. There's considerable more dress here, but I guess, on the whole, it ain't any better a place to live in than Green River."

The three women had not had a very lively or pleasant visit in Elliot. Jane Field, full of grim defiance of her own guilt and misery and of them, was not a successful entertainer of guests. She fed them as best she could with her scanty resources, and after her house-work was done, took her knitting-work and sat with them in her gloomy sitting-room, while they also kept busy at the little pieces of handiwork they had brought with them.

They talked desperately of Green River and the people there; they told Mrs. Field of this one and that one whom she had known, and in whom she had been interested; but she seemed to have forgotten everybody and everything connected with her old life.

"Ida Starr is goin' to marry the minister in October," Mrs. Babcock had said the day but one after their arrival. "You know there was some talk about it before you went away, Mis' Field. You remember hearin' about it, don't you?"

"I guess I don't remember it," said Mrs. Field.

"Don't remember it? Why, Mis' Field, I should think you'd remember that! It was town's talk how she followed him up. Well, she's got him, an' she's been teachin' — you know she had Lois's school — to get money for her weddin' outfit. They say she's got a brown silk dress to be married in, an' a new black silk one too. Should you think the Starrs could afford any such outlay?"

"I dunno as I should," replied Mrs. Field.

When she went out of the room presently, Mrs. Babcock turned to the others. "She didn't act as if she cared no more about it than nothin' at all," she said indignantly. "She don't act to me as if she had any more interest in Green River than Jerusalem, nor the folks that live there. I keep thinkin' I won't tell her another thing about it. I never see anybody so changed as she is."

"Mebbe she ain't well," said Mrs. Green. "I think she looks awfully. She's as thin as a rail, an' she ain't a mite of color. Lois looks better."

"Mis' Field never did have any flesh on her bones," Mrs. Babcock rejoined; "an' as for Lois, nothin' ever did ail her but spring weather an' fussin'. I guess Mis' Field's well enough, but havin' all this property left her has made a different woman of her. I've seen people's noses teeter up in the air when their purses got heavy before now."

"It ain't that," said Amanda.

"What is it, then?" asked Mrs. Babcock sharply.

"I dunno. I know one thing: home's the best place for everybody if they've got one."

"I don't think 'tis always. I b'lieve when you're off on an excursion ticket in makin' the best of things, for my part. To-morrow's Sunday, an' I expect to enjoy the meetin' an' seein' the folks. I shall be kinder glad, for my part, not to see exactly the same old bonnets an' made-over silks that I see every Sunday to home. I like a change sometimes. It puts new ideas into your head, an' I feel as if I had spunk enough to stan' it."

On Sunday Mrs. Field led her procession of guests into church; and they, in their best black gowns and bonnets, sat listening to the sermon, and looking about with decorous and furtive curiosity.

Mrs. Babcock had a handsome fan with spangles on it, and she fanned herself airily, lifting her head up with the innocent importance of a stranger.

She had quite a fine bonnet, and a new mantle with some beaded fringe on it; when she stirred, it tinkled. She looked around and did not see another woman with one as handsome. It was the gala moment of her visit to Elliot. Afterward she was wont to say that when she was in Elliot she did not go out much, nobody came to the house nor anything, but she went to meeting and she enjoyed that.

It was the evening following that Mrs. Jane Maxwell came. Mrs. Field, sitting with her guests, felt a strange contraction of her heart when she heard the door open.

"Who's that comin'?" asked Mrs. Babcock.

"I guess it's old Mr. Maxwell's brother Henry's wife," replied

Mrs. Field.

She arose. Lois went quickly and softly out of the other door. She felt sure that exposure was near, and her first impulse was to be out of sound and hearing of it. She sat there in the dark on the front door-step awhile, then she went into the house. Sitting there in doubt, half hearing what might be dreadful to hear, was worse than certainty. She had at once a benumbing terror and a fierce desire that her mother should be betrayed, and withal a sudden impulse of loyalty toward her, a feeling that she would stand by her when everybody else turned against her.

She crept in and sat down. Mrs. Maxwell was talking to Mrs. Babcock about the state of the church in Elliot. It was wonderful that this call was made without exposure, but it was. Twice Mrs. Maxwell called Jane Field "Esther," but nobody noticed it except Amanda, and she said nothing. She only caught her breath each time with a little gasp.

Mrs. Maxwell addressed herself almost wholly to Mrs. Babcock concerning her daughter, her daughter's husband, and the people of Elliot. Mrs. Babcock constantly bore down upon her, and swerved her aside with her own topics. Indeed, all the conversation lay between these two. There was a curious similarity between them. They belonged apparently to some one subdivision of human nature, being as birds of the same feather, and seemed to instinctively recognize this fact.

They were at once attracted, and regarded each other with a kind of tentative cordiality, which might later become antagonism, for they were on a level for either friendship or enmity.

Mrs. Maxwell made a long call, as she was accustomed to do. She was a frequent visitor, generally coming in the evening, and going home laden with spoil, creeping from cover to cover like a cat. She was afraid to have her daughter and nephew know of all the booty she obtained. She had many things snugly tucked away in bureau drawers and the depths of closets which she had carried home under her shawl by night. Jane Field was only too glad to give her all for which she asked or hinted.

To-night, as Mrs. Maxwell took leave of the three strange women standing in a prim row, she gave a meaning nod to Mrs. Field, who followed her to the door.

"I was thinkin' about that old glass preserve-dish," she whispered. "I don't s'pose it's worth much, but if you don't use it ever, I s'pose I might as well have it. Flora has considerable company now, an' ours ain't a very good size."

When Mrs. Maxwell had gone out of the yard with the heavy

cut-glass dish pressed firmly against her side under her black silk shawl, Jane Field felt like one who had had a reprieve from instant execution, although she had already suffered the slow torture. She went back to her guests as steady-faced as ever. She was quite sure none of them had noticed Mrs. Maxwell's calling her Esther, but her eyes were like a wary animal's as she entered the room, although not a line in her long pale face was unsteady.

The time went on and nobody said, "Why did she call you Esther instead of Jane?"

They seemed as usual. Mrs. Babcock questioned her sharply about Mrs. Maxwell — how much property she had and if her daughter had married well. Amanda never looked in her face, and said nothing, but she was often quiet and engrossed in a new tidy she was knitting.

"They don't suspect," Mrs. Field said to herself.

They were going home the next day but one; she went to bed nearly as secure as she had been for the last three months. Mrs. Maxwell was to be busy the next day — she had spoken of making pear sauce — she would not be in again. The danger of exposure from the coming of these three women to Elliot was probably past. But Jane Field lay awake all night. Suddenly at dawn she formed a plan; her mind was settled. There was seemingly no struggle. It was to her as if she turned a corner, once turned there was no other way, and no question about it. When it was time, she got up, dressed herself, and went about the house, as usual. There was no difference in her look or manner, but all the morning Lois kept glancing at her in a startled, half-involuntary way; then she would look away again, seeing nothing to warrant it, but ere long her eyes turned again toward her mother's face. It was as if she had a subtle consciousness of something there which was beyond vision, and to which her vision gave the lie. When she looked away she saw it again, but it vanished when her eyes were turned, like a black robe through a door.

After dinner, when the dishes were cleared away, the three visitors sat as usual in company state with their needle-work. Amanda's bag upstairs was all neatly packed. She would need to unpack it again that night, but it was a comfort to her. She had scarcely spoken all day; her thin mouth had a set look.

"Mandy's gettin' so homesick she can't speak," said Mrs. Babcock. "She can't hardly wait till to-morrow to start, can you, Mandy?"

"No, I can't," replied Amanda.

Mrs. Field was in her bedroom changing her dress when Lois

put on her hat and went down the street with some finished work for the dressmaker for whom she sewed.

"Where you goin', Lois?" asked Mrs. Babcock, when she came through the room with her hat on.

"I'm going out a little ways," answered Lois evasively. She had tried to keep the fact of her sewing for a living from the Green River women. She knew how people in Elliot talked about it, and estranged as she was from her mother, she wanted no more reflections cast upon her.

But Mrs. Babcock peeped out of a window as Lois went down the path. "She's got a bundle," she whispered. "I tell you what 'tis, I suspect that girl is sewin' for somebody to earn money. I should think her mother would be ashamed of herself."

Lois had a half mile to walk, and she stayed awhile at the dressmaker's to sew. When she started homeward it was nearly three o'clock.

It was a beautiful afternoon, the house yards were full of the late summer flowers, the fields were white and gold with arnica and wild-carrot instead of buttercups and daisies, the blackberries were ripe along the road-side, and there were sturdy thickets of weeds picked out with golden buttons of tansy over the stone walls. Lois stepped along lightly. She did not look like the same girl of three months ago. It was strange that in spite of all her terrible distress of mind and hard struggles since she came to Elliot it should have been so, but it was. Every life has its own conditions, although some are poisons. Whether it had been as Mrs. Babcock thought, that the girl had been afflicted with no real malady, only the languor of the spring, intensified and fostered in some subtle fashion by her mother's anxiety, or whether it had been the purer air of Elliot that had brought about the change, to whatever it might have been due, she was certainly better.

Lois had on an old pink muslin dress that she had worn many a summer, indeed the tucks had been let down to accord with her growth, and showed in bars of brighter pink around the skirt. But the color of the dress became her well, her young shoulders filled out the thin fabric with sweet curves that overcame the old fashion of its make; her slender arms showed through the sleeves; and her small fair face was set in a muslin frill like a pink corolla. She had to pass the cemetery on her way home. As she came in sight of its white shafts, and headstones gleaming out from its dark foliage, she met Francis Arms. She started when she saw him, and said, "Good-afternoon" nervously; then was passing on, but he stopped her.

"Where are you going?" he asked.

"I was going home."

"See here — I don't know as you want to — but — do you remember how we went to walk in the cemetery that first day after you came?"

Lois nodded. He could see only the tip of her chin under her broad hat.

"Suppose — if you haven't anything else to do — if you are not busy — that we go in there now a little ways?" said Francis.

"I guess I'd better not," replied Lois, in a trembling voice.

"It's real cool in there."

"I'm afraid I'd better not."

"Well," said Francis, "of course I won't tease you if you don't want to."

He tried to make his tone quite unconcerned and to smile. He was passing on, but Lois spoke.

"I might go in there just a minute," she said.

Francis turned quickly, his face lighted up. They walked along together to the cemetery gate; he opened it and they entered and passed slowly down the drive-way.

The yard was largely overhung by evergreen trees, which held in their boughs cool masses of blue gloom. It was cool there, as Francis had said, although it was quite a warm day. The flowers on the sunny graves hung low, unless they had been freshly tended, when they stood erect in dark circles. Some of the old uncared-for graves were covered with rank growths of grass and weeds, which seemed fairly instinct with merry life this summer afternoon. Crickets and cicadas thrilled through them; now and then a bird flew up. It was like a resurrection stir.

"Let's go where we went that first day," said Francis; "it's always pleasant there on the bank."

Lois followed him without a word. They sat down on the grass at the edge of the terrace, and a cool breeze came in their faces from over the great hollow of the meadows below. The grass on them had been cut short, and now had dried and turned a rosy color in the sun. The two kept their eyes turned away from each other, and looked down into the meadow as into the rosy hollow of a cup; but they seemed to see each other's faces there.

"It's cool here, isn't it?" said Francis.

"Real cool."

"It always is on the hottest day. There is always a breeze here, if there isn't anywhere else."

Francis's words were casual, but his voice was unsteady with a tender tone that seemed to overweight it.

Lois seemed to hear only this tone, and not the words. It was one of the primitive tones that came before any language was made, and related to the first necessities of man. Suddenly she had ears for that only. She did not say anything. Her hands were folded in her lap quietly, but her fingers tingled.

"Lois," Francis began; then he stopped.

Lois did not look up.

"See here, Lois," he went on, "I don't know as there is much use in my saying anything. You've hardly noticed me lately. There was one spell when I thought maybe — But — Well, I'm going to ask you, and have it over with one way or the other. Lois, do you think — well, do you feel as if you could ever — marry me some time?"

Lois dropped her head down on her hands.

"Now don't you go to feeling bad if you can't," said Francis. "It won't be your fault. But if you'd just tell me, Lois."

Lois did not speak.

"If you'd just tell me one way or the other, Lois."

"I can't. I can't anyway!" cried Lois then, with a great sob.

"Well, if you can't, don't cry, little girl. There's nothing to cry about. I can stand it. All the trouble is, it does seem to me that I could take care of you better than any other fellow on earth, but maybe that's my conceit, and you'll find somebody else that will do better than I. Now don't cry." Francis pulled her hat off gently, and patted her head. His face was quite white, but he tried to smile. "Don't cry, dear," he said again. "It was nothing you could help. I didn't much suppose you liked me. There's nothing much in me to like. I'm an ordinary kind of a fellow."

Francis got up and walked off a little way.

Lois sobbed harder. Finally she stole a glance at him between her fingers. She could see his profile quite pale and stern as he stood on the edge of the terrace. She made a little inarticulate call, and he turned quickly.

"What is it, Lois?" he asked, coming toward her.

"I didn't say — I — didn't like you," she whispered faintly.

"Lois!"

"I didn't say so."

"Lois, do you? Answer me quick."

She hid her face again.

"Lois, you must answer me now."

"I like you well enough, but I can't marry you."

"Lois, is there any fellow in Green River that wants you? Is that the reason?"

She shook her head. "I can't ever marry anybody," she said, and her voice was suddenly quite firm. She wiped her eyes.

Francis sat down beside her. "O Lois, you do love me, after all?"

"I can't marry you," said she.

"Why not, dear?"

"I can't. You mustn't ask me why."

Francis looked down at her half laughing. "Some dreadful obstacle in the way?"

She nodded solemnly.

Francis put his arm around her. "Oh, my dear," he said, "don't you know obstacles go for nothing if you do like me, after all? Wait a little and you'll find out. O Lois, are you sure you do like me? You are so pretty."

"I can't," repeated Lois, trembling.

"Suppose this obstacle were removed, dear, you would then?"

"It never can be."

"But if it were, you would? Yes, of course you would. Then I shall remove it, you depend upon it, I shall, dear. Lois, I liked you the minute I saw you, and, it's terribly conceited, but I do believe you liked me a little. Dear, if it ever can be, I'll take care of you all my life."

The two sat there together, and the long summer afternoon passed humming and singing with bees and birds, and breathing sweetly through the pine branches. They themselves were as a fixed heart of love in the midst of it, and all around them in their graves lay the dead who had known and gone beyond it all, but nobody could tell if they had forgotten.

CHAPTER X

When Lois left home that afternoon her mother had been in her bedroom changing her dress. When she came out she had on her best black dress, her black shawl and gloves, and her best bonnet. The three women stared at her. She stood before them a second without speaking. The strange look, for which Lois had watched her face, had appeared.

"Why, what is the matter, Mis' Field?" cried Mrs. Babcock. "Where be you going?"

"I'm goin' out a little ways," replied Mrs. Field. Then she raised her voice suddenly. "I've got something to say to all of you before I go," said she. "I've been deceivin' you, and everybody here in Elliot. When I came down here, they all took me for my sister, Esther Maxwell, and I let them think so. They've all called me Esther Maxwell here. That's how I got the money. Old Mr. Maxwell left it to Flora Maxwell if my sister didn't outlive him. I shouldn't have had a cent. I stole it. I thought my daughter would die if we didn't have it an' get away from Green River; but that wa'n't any excuse. Edward Maxwell had that fifteen hundred dollars of my husband's, an' I never had a cent of it; but that wa'n't any excuse. I thought I'd jest stay here an' carry it out till I got the money back; but that wa'n't any excuse. I ain't spent a cent of the money; it's all put away just as it was paid in, in a sugar-bowl in the china closet; but that ain't any excuse. I took it on myself to do justice instead of the Lord, an' that ain't for any human bein' to do. I ain't Esther Maxwell. I'm brought up short. I ain't Esther Maxwell!" Her voice rose to a stern shriek.

The three women stared at her, then at each other. Their faces were white. Amanda was catching her breath in faint gasps. Jane Field rushed out of the room. The door closed heavily after her.

Three wild, pale faces huddled together in a window watched her out of the yard. Mrs. Babcock called weakly after her to come back, but she kept on. She went out of the yard and down the street. At the first house she stopped, went up to the door and rang the bell. When a woman answered her ring, she looked at her and said, "I ain't Esther Maxwell!" Then she turned and went down the walk between the rows of marigolds and asters, and the woman stood staring after her for a minute, then ran in, and the windows filled with wondering faces.

Jane Field stopped at the next house with the same message. After she left a woman pelted across the yard in a panic to compare notes with her neighbors. She kept on down the street, and she stopped at every door and said, "I ain't Esther Maxwell."

Now and then somebody tried to delay her to question her and obtain an explanation, but she broke away. There was about her a terrible mental impetus which intimidated. People stood instinctively out of her way, as before some rushing force which might overwhelm them.

Daniel Tuxbury followed her out to the street; then he fell back. Mrs. Jane Maxwell caught hold of her dress, but she let go, and leaned trembling over her iron gate looking after the relentless black figure speeding to the next door.

She went on and on, all the summer afternoon, and canvassed the little village with her remorse and confession of crime. Finally the four words which she said at the doors seemed almost involuntary. They became her one natural note, the expression of her whole life. It was as if she had never said any others. At last, going along the street, she repeated them to everybody she met. Some she had told before, but she did not know it. She said them to a little girl in a white frock, with her hair freshly curled, carrying a doll, and she ran away crying with fright. She said them to three barefooted boys loping along in the dust, with berry-pails, and they laughed and turned around and mocked her, calling the words after her. When she went up the path to the Maxwell house, she said them where the shadow of a pine-tree fell darkly in front of her like the shadow of a man. She said them when she stood before the door of the house whose hospitality she had usurped. There was a little crowd at her heels, but she did not notice them until she was entering the door. Then she said the words over to them: "I ain't Esther Maxwell."

She entered the sitting-room, the people following. There were her three old friends and neighbors, the minister and his wife, Daniel Tuxbury, his sister and her daughter, Mrs. Jane Maxwell and her daughter, and her own Lois. She faced them all and said it again: "I ain't Esther Maxwell."

The lawyer jerked himself forward; his face was twitching. "This woman's mind is affected," he declared with loud importance. "She is Esther Maxwell. I will swear to it in any court. I recognize her, and I never forget a face."

"I ain't Esther Maxwell," said Jane Field, in her voice that was as remorseless and conclusive as fate.

Lois pressed forward and clung to her.

"Mother!" she moaned; "mother!"

Then for once her mother varied her set speech. "Lois wa'n't to blame," she said; "I want you to know it, all of you. Lois wa'n't to blame. She didn't know until after I'd done it. She wanted to tell, but I told her they'd put me in prison. Lois wa'n't to blame. I ain't Esther Maxwell."

"O mother, don't, don't!" Lois sobbed.

She hung about her mother's neck, and pressed her lips to that pale wrinkled face, whose wrinkles seemed now to be laid in stone. Not a muscle of Jane Field's face changed. She kept repeating at intervals, in precisely the same tone, her terrible under-chord to all the excitement about her: "I ain't Esther Maxwell."

Some of the women were crying. Amanda Pratt sat sewing fast, with her mouth set. She clung to her familiar needle as if it were a rope to save her from destruction. Francis Arms had come in, and stood close to Lois and her mother.

Suddenly Jane Maxwell spoke. She was pale, and her head-dress was askew.

"I call this pretty work," said she.

Then Mrs. Babcock faced her. "I should call it pretty work for somebody else besides poor Mis' Field," she cried. "I'd like to know what business your folks had takin' her money an' keepin' it. She wa'n't goin' to take any more than belonged to her, an' she had a perfect right to, accordin' to my way of thinkin'."

Mrs. Maxwell gasped. Flora laid her hand on her arm when she tried to speak again.

"I'm goin' to tell her how I've been without a decent dress, an' how I've been luggin' my own things out of this house, an' now I've got to lug 'em all back again," she whispered defiantly.

"Mother, you keep still," said Flora.

Mrs. Green went across the room and put her arm around Lois, standing by her mother. "Let's you an' me get her in her bedroom, an' have her lay down on the bed, an' try an' quiet her," she whispered. "She's all unstrung. Mebbe she'll be better."

Mrs. Field at once turned toward her.

"I ain't Esther Maxwell," said she.

"O Mis' Field! oh, poor woman! it ain't for us to judge you," returned Mrs. Green, in her tender, inexpressibly solemn voice. "Come, Lois."

"Yes, that'll be a good plan," chimed in Mrs. Babcock. "She'd better go in her bedroom where it's quiet, or she'll wind up with a fever. There's too many folks here."

"I wonder if some of my currant wine wouldn't be good for her?" said Mrs. Jane Maxwell, with an air of irrepressible virtue.

"She don't want none of your currant wine," rejoined Mrs. Babcock fiercely. "She's suffered enough by your family."

"I guess you needn't be so mighty smart," returned Mrs. Maxwell, jerking her arm away from Flora. "I dunno of anything she's suffered. I should think Flora an' me had been the ones to suffer, an' now we shan't never go to law, nor make any fuss about it. I ain't goin' to stay here an' be talked to so any longer if I know, especially by folks that ain't got any business meddlin' with it, anyway. I suppose this is my daughter's house, an' I've got a perfect right in it, but I'm a-goin'."

Mrs. Jane Maxwell went out, her ribbons and silken draperies fluttering as if her own indignation were a wind, but Flora stayed.

The women led Jane Field into her little bedroom, took off her bonnet and shawl and dress as if she were dead, and made her lie down. They bathed her head with camphor, they plied her with soothing arguments, but she kept on her one strain. She was singularly docile in all but that. Mrs. Green dropped on her knees beside the bed and prayed. When she said amen, Jane Field called out her confession as if in the ear of God. They sent for the doctor and he gave her a soothing draught, and she slept. The women watched with her, as ever and anon she stirred and murmured in her sleep, "I ain't Esther Maxwell." And she said it when she first awoke in the morning.

"She's sayin' it now," whispered Mrs. Babcock to Mrs. Green, "and I believe she'll say it her whole life."

And Jane Field did. The stern will of the New England woman had warped her whole nature into one groove. Gradually she seemed more like herself, and her mind was in other respects apparently clear, but never did she meet a stranger unless she said for greeting, "I ain't Esther Maxwell."

And she said it to her own daughter on her wedding-day, when she came in her white dress from the minister's with Francis. The new joy in Lois's face affected her like the face of a stranger, and she turned on her and said, "I ain't Esther Maxwell."

THE END